GONE STEADY

KATRINA MARIE

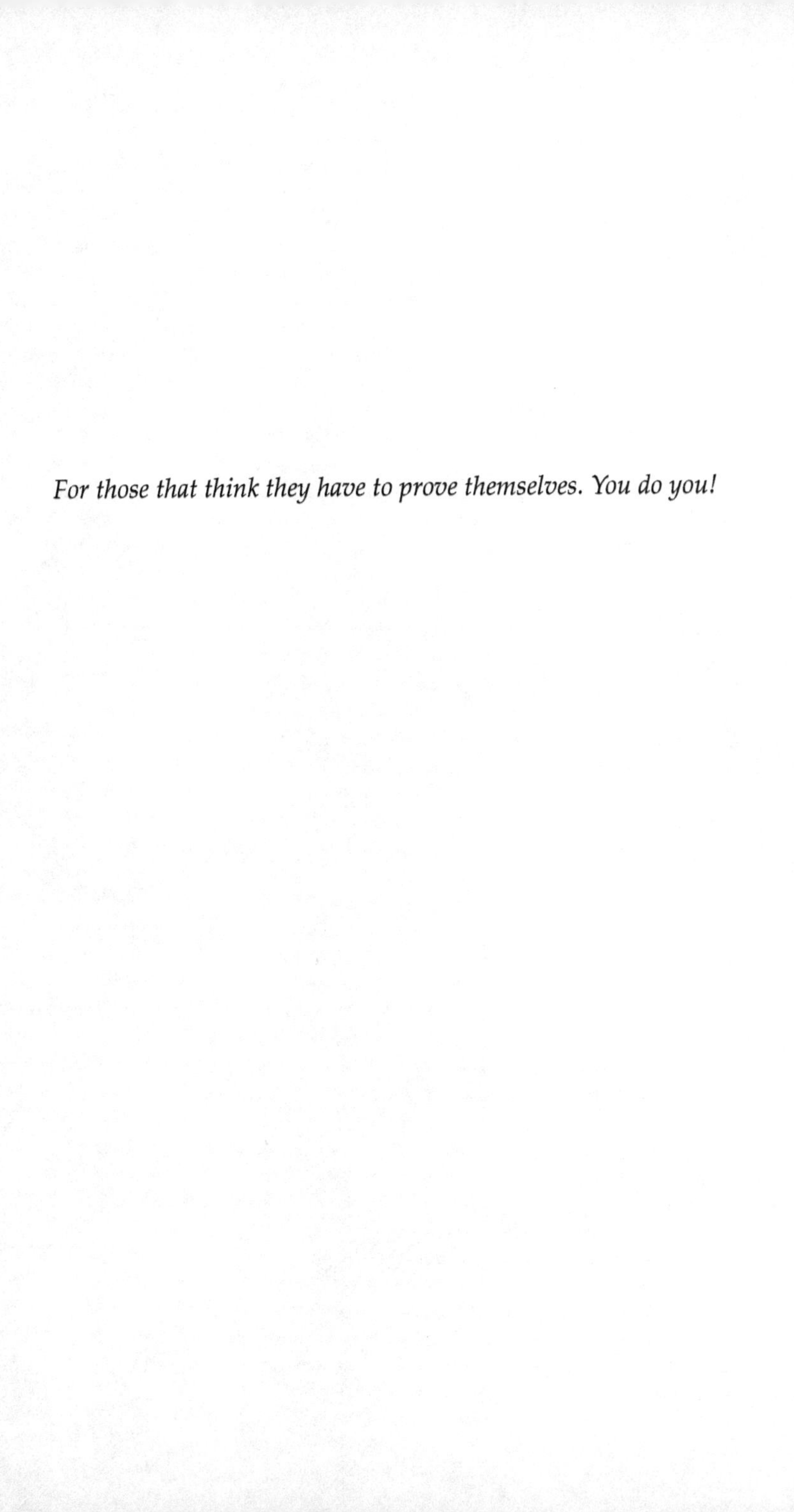

For those that think they have to prove themselves. You do you!

ONE

Tiffany

THE BASS IS THRUMMING through my body as people press against each other. The music flows through the crowd. This is my happy place. The only thing that would make this better is if Audrey and Stella were here tonight. Stella, of course, couldn't make it because she had to get into a committed relationship. Don't get me wrong, she deserves all the happiness in the world and I am truly happy for her. But, did she have to fall for a guy four hours away? She can't join me on my spur of the moment adventures anymore. Audrey, on the other hand, bailed on me and is lame. I get this isn't her scene, so I don't blame her completely.

I just need them here to keep my crazy ass in line. Hopefully, they're busy finding a roommate. The last few they've picked have been complete duds. They need to stop thinking about what their likes and dislikes are and start thinking about what works for me. It is too bad I can't be trusted to pick my own damn roommate. My bullshit radar is on the fritz, and the last few people I've moved into my apartment have been horrible choices.

The band on stage plays a cover of "The Imperial March," and as much as I don't care for Star Wars, I can't deny that the rock edge they put on it is amazing. It's enough to have me acting like a damn fool jumping up and down. This is what I live for. Getting lost in the music and giving up any worry I have over living up to the same expectations as my cousins. If my mom or dad mentions how proud they are of my cousins one more time, I will lose my shit. As the band switches to a cover of Nirvana, I sing at the top of my lungs. Putting all my frustration at being the family screwup into every single word.

Being serious is overrated. I love my life. I only need to live up to my own expectations and flutter wherever the wind takes me. It may have caused me to make a few bad decisions along the way, but I don't regret any of them. Who needs a steady nine-to-five job? Not me. I won't be happy in that environment. And if I had that job, my ass wouldn't be at a concert on a weeknight, having an incredible time.

Someone bumps into me from behind causing me to fall to the ground. Suddenly all my doom and gloom thoughts are gone and I am pissed.

A man looms over me, his lips moving, but I can't hear what he's saying.

"What?" I scream above the roaring crowd.

He bends closer, his eyes hidden behind square black frames, brows furrowed. "Are you hurt?" He holds his hand out to help me up, taking me by surprise.

"I—I don't think so," I reach for his hand and allow him to pull me up. "You kind of came out of nowhere."

"I'm so sorry," he brings me closer to him so he doesn't have to yell. "I didn't mean to plow you over. The assholes back there are being kinda pushy."

Most girls would be uncomfortable so close to someone they don't know. Not me. All I want to do is get to know him a little better. The way his plain white t-shirt molds to his body is perfection. "It's okay." He opens his mouth to protest, but I cut him off. "We are in the pit. The likelihood of me getting jostled around is pretty high." I stare at him for emphasis.

"Jostled and getting your ass knocked to the ground are two very different things." His dark brown eyes study me. *What is he looking for?*

"Seriously, I'm good." I turn back toward the stage, ready to rock out. This guy is cute and all but he can't give me the high music gives me. Not yet, anyway. After a few more drinks, that may change.

Tap. Tap. Tap. A finger raps on my shoulder. "Are you sure?" I'm not even fully facing him before the words are out of his mouth.

Do I blow him off? This is the big question of the night. He's not too shabby to look at, and he's kind, if not a little too kind. "If you really want to make it up to me, you can buy me a drink." I'm not above getting free drinks.

"I can definitely do that." He walks toward the bar area, and stops. "Want to come with me?"

Not really. I love this band, and I don't want to miss any part of their set. But he was nice enough to help me up after knocking me over. Not to mention the fact that I've seen this band almost ten times, prompts me to hook my arm into his. "Sure."

We push our way through the crowd, trying to keep from getting jostled around. It shouldn't be this hard to get out of the pit. It never has been before. The fans are amped up, though. It'll be almost impossible for us to get back in the area we just left.

"What's your name?" My new, bespectacled friend asks. His mouth is near my ear to be heard over the crowd, and a shiver runs down my spine. I'd be lying if I said that's never happened before. I'm no stranger to lust, and this guy fits the bill.

"Tiffany," I yell, unsure if he can hear me over the roar of the crowd.

Finally, we get to the exit. Once we leave the main concert area, the noise is down and everything feels muted. It's crazy how one thick wall can change the sound of everything, even in an open air venue. "What's your name?" My voice is louder than necessary, still adjusting the quieter atmosphere.

He chuckles and removes his arm from mine. Nobody has ever done that before, and the rejection stings. "It's Spencer."

"Do you live in Austin?"

"Yeah," he leads us toward the closest vendor. "I've lived here all my life." The woman behind the counter asks for our ID's. "What do you want to drink?"

"I'm not picky, you choose." Neither one of my cousins could do that. They typically drink the same thing no matter where they go. However, Stella has been broadening her horizons since she started working at that bar in Asheville. It is hilarious because she's acting like these drinks are new just because she's never had them before.

"You're pretty brave," he grins. "I could pick out something horrible for you to drink and you wouldn't even know it."

I shrug my shoulders and lean against the sticky counter. "I guess it's a good thing I know what most of these beers taste like."

"Very clever," he taps me on the nose and orders our drinks. "Back to our earlier conversation."

Shit, what were we talking about.
"Do you live in the area?"
Oh, right. We were talking about living in Austin.

The band starts a new song and a part of me is itching to go back to the pit, but this guy is nice. It wouldn't be a horrible decision to see where tonight may lead. I'm not getting any bad vibes off of him, so all is good. "Yep. I've lived here for a few years."

"What made you pick Austin?"

"My cousins." It's as simple as that. Stella was already here, but when Audrey moved, it just made sense. I didn't want to be stuck in our small town by myself, and moving to a big city seemed like a good thing to do. The adventures I could have here were endless.

"Most people try to get away from their families, not run to them," he laughs.

"They're my best friends. Being around them and seeing them all the time is fun. Until they get all judge-y and get on my nerves. Even then, I love them and can't imagine being away from them. Now, it's kind of boring since my oldest cousin moved away. Audrey doesn't like to go to these things unless Stella is with us."

"That's a shame." He shakes his head and looks toward the crowd we were just in. "If you ever need someone to join you for live music, I'm available."

Whoah. Wait a hot damn minute. Is he trying to ask me on future dates, or is he just making small talk to make me feel better? I'm not that type of girl. I don't do multiple dates, at least not for long. I know that one statement shouldn't shake me up this much, but my good sense is being distracted by his looks and how easy he is to talk to.

"We'll see." I shrug, hoping the answer is as noncommittal as possible. I wouldn't be opposed to seeing him again, but I plan for concerts months in advance. Hell, I had tickets for my cousins for this one since before Stella moved to nowheresville. Then, Stella couldn't make it because she was busy with her new job in Asheville, and Audrey bailed last minute, naturally.

We grab our beers and instead of returning to the pit, we find an open spot on the lawn. It's easier to talk up here while enjoying the music. "So, what do you do for a living?"

"I'm a waitress at a restaurant downtown." I wait for the look of horror to cross his face, or for him to decide that I don't have any aspirations. You'd be surprised how many times I'm asked when I will get a real job. For me, this is a real job. I enjoy what I do, and I don't think I should make apologies for it.

To my surprise, he doesn't say one bad thing. "How do you not get tired standing in the pit after you've been on your feet all day?"

"It's an entirely different energy when I'm at a concert."

"That makes sense," he nods. We watch the rest of the show in silence, soaking up the music and enjoying the night air. Once the band is finishes their encore song, we stay seated while everyone gets up in droves to walk to their cars. "Did you drive here?"

"No, I took an Uber. I don't want to drive if there's a chance I'll be drinking." I grab my phone to let Audrey know the show is over. She may not be here, but I at least like to let her know I'm safe.

"Any chance you want to grab something to eat with me?" His eyes are on the ground while he asks, unsure of what I'll say.

"Sure," I say. "How do pancakes sound?"

We get up and walk to the exit of the venue. "I'll get us a ride."

"Thanks." Phone still in hand, I send a group text to Audrey and Stella.

Tiffany: Concert is done. Having dinner with a fellow concert goer.
Stella: Is he hot?
Tiffany: Who said it was a "he"?
Audrey: Because when isn't it a he?
Tiffany: You have a point.
Audrey: Turn on your location sharing so I know you're safe.
Tiffany: Yes, Mom.
Stella: Have fun. Don't do anything I wouldn't do.
Tiffany: Do you know who you're talking to? Besides, it's not like I'll ever see him again.
Audrey: I'm not kidding. TURN IT ON!
Stella: You better do it. Call me tomorrow with all the details. Also, I put out another ad on a roommate for you.
Tiffany: You got it.

I turn on the location sharing on my phone. If I don't Audrey will bug the hell out of me until I do. I can't have her cramping my style tonight. I have every intention of going home with this guy.

The Uber he requested pulls up to the curb. "After you," he opens the door and I slide into the backseat. He sits beside me instead of the front seat, and I know he's definitely interested. "Want to get those pancakes to go?"

TWO

Spencer

HOLY CRAP. How do I answer that? This is new territory for me. I don't do hookups. Hell, I don't date. Nobody likes the nerdy guy. Not that I think I'm hideous or anything, but usually as soon as comic or movie facts burst out of my mouth, they run away. Plus, if they ever saw my apartment, they'd never come back. I'll blame talking to her on liquid courage. There is *no way* I would have been able to talk to a force of nature like her without it.

I can just tell she lives life fearlessly and does whatever she wants. In all the concerts I've been to with my friends, I've never seen a woman hang out in the pit by herself. Let alone, feel confident that she'll be okay.

"Spencer?" Her voices breaks into my thoughts.

"Huh?"

"The pancakes? Are you good with getting them to go?"

Oh, right. I forgot I'm the one who initiated this whole eating thing. Even worse, where are we supposed to go after we pick up the food? She didn't offer her place, so I guess it is my apartment then. "Sure."

"Look guys," the Uber driver speaks up. "I just need to know where you want me to go."

"Actually pancakes would be a horrible idea," Tiffany sits up straighter. "Run us through the nearest drive through, please. Then, Spencer can decide where to go from there."

"I can do that," the driver says and puts the vehicle in drive.

The car is deadly silent aside from the low music coming from the speakers. A stark contrast from the loud concert we just left. Fear courses through me. She's going to realize just how awkward I am, and bail. Not that I'd blame her.

Tiffany is looking out the window, taking in the city she lives in. "You look at your surroundings like you've never seen them before."

She shrugs her shoulders, and keeps staring. "I've lived here for a few years, but it seems like there is always something new to see. A new adventure that opens up." She glances at me no doubt seeing my confusion. "It's just a lot different in the town I grew up in."

"You're very spirited in the way you describe things."

"Try living in a place where you have expectations to do things a certain way, and everything closes before ten at night." She turns to me. "You start taking chances and doing what makes you happy."

There's a lot more to this woman than I thought. Maybe she isn't just a party girl. She could be the one who doesn't laugh at my obsession over comic books.

The driver pulls into *Whataburger*. "I'll pull up to the speaker where your window is."

"Sounds good," Tiffany beams, still somehow full of energy.

As soon as we're at the speaker, I roll down the back-seat window, and turn to Tiffany. "What do you want?"

She taps her finger against her chin. "Um, a large fry and chocolate shake."

I nod my head and turn toward the static voice coming through. "I need two large french fries, a regular chocolate shake, and large Dr. Pepper."

The person working the drive thru gives me the total and we pull forward. "Can you ask for spicy ketchup when we get up there?"

"Sure," I shrug. "It really is the best ketchup out there. They just never give enough."

"Maybe you should ask for a specific amount."

"Good idea."

The Uber driver stops with the back window in front of the drive thru window, and I hand my card over to pay despite Tiffany's objections while she digs through her small bag. "You can stop looking. I already paid."

"Thanks," she breathes and relief washes over her face.

Our food now taking up the small space between us, the driver asks where we're heading next. I rattle off my address, and don't miss the way Tiffany's shoulders sag. I'm not sure if it's from disappointment or relief, but I'm not going to question it. The car is already following the path on GPS , and I don't want to annoy our driver more than we already have.

He pulls up to the house, and Tiffany gasps. "This is your house," she almost yells as she gets out of the car.

"Thanks, Man," I tell the driver as I grab the bag contenting our food and shut the door. "No. My place is the apartment above the garage. But we have to be quiet I don't want to wake the landlords." I'm not going to mention they are also my parents. As soon as I graduated from college, I came back home. Not willing to live in the house, I asked if I could move into the small apartment over the garage. She doesn't need to know all that, though. Not unless she actually sticks around.

"Oh," she covers her mouth. "Sorry. I didn't realize."

"It's okay." Grabbing her hand, I start walking toward the stairs that lead to the apartment. She doesn't pull away. I wasn't sure if she'd balk at me grabbing her, but I'm going off of what I've seen in movies. The few girlfriends I've had were like me, and awkward as hell. I should have grabbed another drink before they stopped serving it at the concert. I'm losing my buzz…and my bravado. *Come on alcohol. Stick with me just a little longer.*

"Can you hold onto these for a second? The door can be a little tricky." She nods, and I hand off the bag holding our food and my drink. Pulling the key out of my pocket, I insert it into the door knob. Nothing happens when I turn it, and it's going to be one of those nights. I really should replace this door. The only plus side is my parents haven't figure out how to get it unstuck, and I don't want to get rid of that small piece of privacy.

With my hand still on the key, I use the other one to pull the door toward me and lift up. Turning the key quickly, the lock release and the door swings open. Hopefully there isn't a mess in there.

Grabbing the bag and cup from her hand, I gesture for her to go in ahead of me. I flip the light switch on as soon as she's through the door, and follow her. "Wow," she turns in a circle, taking in the small space. "You have quite the obsession."

Is that a good thing, or bad thing? I can't tell from her expression. But she comes toward, taking the food and drink from me and sets them on the small table in the middle of the room. My eyes widen and I blurt out, "Aren't we going to eat?"

"Later." She clearly has one thing on her mind, and I may be awkward as hell, but I'm not stupid. Tiffany is actually interested in me, despite seeing the posters all over my walls. And I'm more than interested in her. She's funny, energetic, and everything I could possibly want in a woman. Who cares if I just met her.

She wraps her arms around my neck, leans forward and presses small kisses along my throat. Then my jawline until her lips reach my mouth. Her tongue sweeps across the seam of my lips, and I grant her entrance. *Stay calm. You've had sex before. This isn't anything new. Don't freak out.*

Her hands slide down my chest and stop at the edge of my shirt, her mouth never leaving mine. She wasn't lying when she said she goes after what she wants. I wish I could be more like her. But even now, with her doing all the work, I'm barely holding onto my sanity. She lifts my shirt up, breaking the kiss long enough to pull it over my head, and grabs the hem of her shirt tossing it near mine.

I ignore my hammering heart, and pull her toward me. I can't let her think I'm a complete loser. Even though, deep inside, that's what I feel like. I still live on my parent's property for crying out loud. Tiffany left her small town and moved hours away to a city she didn't know much about.

Crashing my mouth down on hers, I reach around her, fumbling with her bra. Shit, they make these things impossible to take off even if you're looking directly at it. Her fingers unlatch the button of my jeans and begins shoving them down. I help by moving my feet bringing them down faster. But, this stupid bra is giving me hell.

Tiffany pulls back and grins. "Need some help?" She

reaches her arms behind her and the bra is unclasped in less than two seconds.

"How in the world did you do that?" I can't keep the awe out of my voice. Women must have magical super powers.

"I've had to wear a bra since I was like twelve," she laughs. "It's pretty much second nature. Now, less talking and more kissing." She leads me to the couch along the wall by the door and pushes me down.

She undoes the button on her own pants, and slides them off, taking her panties with them. She is fucking glorious and I can't look away. Stalking toward me as if I'm her prey, she sits on my lap. Legs straddling either side of me. My breath hitches and I can't believe this gorgeous woman is interested in *me*. "Do you want to keep going?"

I nod my head vigorously. Who in their right mind would turn this woman down? Nobody, that's who.

"Good," she smiles and kisses me once again. Even though I didn't hide my interest in her when I was drinking, now I feel like that lonely virgin nerd I was in high school. Dumbfounded when someone showed any sort of interest in me. Not overthinking things any longer, I place my hands on her face and deepen the kiss.

She needs to know that I can actually be more than what I appear. That I won't be content letting her do all the work. But one thing is for sure, this couch is not big enough to do much of anything. Moving one hand down to the small of her back, I pull her closer to me, and stand up. Her arms grip my neck tighter, and her mouth works against my jawline and nibbles on my ear as I make my way toward the room and my bed.

I almost drop her at the new sensation. Nobody has ever done that before. Well, not the way she does it with her tongue sliding against my earlobe before gently biting down. My dick grows harder, and son of a bitch, ears should not be this sensitive.

Finally in my room, I lower her to my bed. Her fiery red hair spread out like a halo on my dark sheets. She may look like an angel, but the way she's biting on her bottom lip and looking at me is a sign of just how much of a temptress she really is. She brings out a reaction in me that nobody has before, and I don't want this night to end.

Shucking off my boxers, I hover over her before she pulls me down on top of her. She wraps her legs around me, and twists, forcing me to roll over until she is on top. Bending down she whispers, "Do you have a condom?"

I nod and point toward the nightstand beside my bed. "In there."

Her body leaves mine for a minute and I take deep breaths, trying to regain some sort of control. If I don't relax, I'm not going to last more than a few minutes.

I hear Tiffany rip open the condom wrapper, and seconds later her hands are sliding it over my erection. My body jerks and she climbs on top of me once again.

The way she's approached me since we arrived at my place seems like she's done this before…a lot. However, the thought floats away as she slides onto my dick, and I can't think of anything else but making sure she comes before I completely blow it.

THE SUN SHINES through the small crack in my curtains, and I want to staple the stupid thing shut. Then, I remember the gorgeous redhead in my bed. As I slide my arm over searching for her body, all I feel is the empty space.

What the hell? Where could she have gone? Stumbling out of bed, I search for my boxers, finding them on the other side of the room. I slide them on and bask in the thoughts of what happened between me and Tiffany. Last night was a whirlwind of sex. When we finally ate our food from *Whataburger*, the fries were cold and her shake was a melted mess. We ended up tossing most of it before climbing back in bed for another round of the most amazing sex I think I've ever had.

The bedroom door is open, and I could have sworn I closed it last night. There's a small possibility it slipped my mind, but not likely. I peek around the door, looking for the woman who blew my mind, but I don't see her. The only closed off area of the space is my bedroom and bathroom, but I know she isn't in either one of those places. She left. Just like that. No goodbye or anything. We didn't even exchange phone numbers.

I search the apartment for a note, something to let me know that last night wasn't a dream. That the girl who is unapologetically herself actually exists. The only evidence I have is our bag of food sitting on top of the full trashcan, and her lacy bra halfway under the couch. I can't believe she left without saying anything. I thought we had a connection while we were at the concert. I thought she felt a zing, too.

Looking around my apartment, I sigh. It was all the comic posters. They drove her away just like I knew they would. Or maybe it's the fact that I live above the garage? I'm not sure what the deal is, but I can't help feeling like shit. I have to do something to get out of this place and on my own. Maybe I will look for a roommate, because I'm not sure I'm capable of living fully on my own just yet.

Sighing, I grab my laptop off of the counter. The only way I'm going to get any woman to take me seriously is if I grow up, and stop acting like a nerdy child. I can do my programming work from anywhere. I just need to find a place to live that isn't my parents' backyard.

I plop onto the couch and open up my laptop. Once everything is loaded, I search for apartments here in the city. I like being close to everything, and I don't want to give that up.

A listing that was posted just yesterday catches my eye. I'd have my own room, and it says that males are preferred. This better not be some cougar trying to get a younger guy to live with her. If it is, it will be a hard no for me. But another requirement makes me pause. *Must agree not to touch food that isn't theirs.* Relief floods through me. Only a dude would be that particular about a roommate.

One last look around the room, and I sigh. I'll apply for this apartment. How bad could it really be?

THREE

Tiffany

MY FIFTH ALARM is going off, and I want to press the snooze button one more time, but I'm supposed to meet Stella, Johnny and Audrey in twenty minutes. I don't even have time for a proper shower. I turn the alarm off and roll out of bed. It's a good thing I keep a large supply of dry shampoo for these occasions.

My phone pings before I make it to my closet, and I check the message. It's the one between me and my cousins the other night.

Audrey: Are you up?
Tiffany: Yep. Getting dressed now.
Stella: You just rolled out of bed, didn't you?
Tiffany: I've been up for hours.
Audrey: Liar. You're probably shacked up at some guy's house.
Tiffany: Nope. I woke up in my own bed. Thank you very much.
Stella: Speaking of guys... What happened with the dude from the concert.

Do I really want to tell them? I've never kept my conquests a secret from them, but there's just something about Spencer, and I want to keep him all to myself. A part of me wishes I had left a note with my number. I actually got along with him, and wouldn't be too disappointed if we hung out again. I guess I'll never know since I crept out of his apartment before the sun even came up.

Tiffany: We had amazing sex.
Stella: Go girl.
Audrey: Don't encourage her. I hope your safe when you meet these guys.
Tiffany: I'm not a moron.
Audrey: I wasn't implying that you are.
Tiffany: If you say so.
Stella: Not going down this road today. Have you left yet, Tiff? We're almost there.
Tiffany: Yep. See you in a few.

They don't need to know that I'm not even dressed. I'll get there soon after they do. I'm the closest to the restaurant, and they don't realize my ninja skills at getting ready quickly.

"You know this talk didn't require a visit, right?" My cousins and Johnny are sitting across from me while we eat brunch. It's taken a while getting used to Johnny being around. For so long it's been just the three of us and it's weird having him as a staple when we get together. Though, he makes Stella happy, and that's all I care about.

"I know," Stella grabs her Bloody Mary and takes a sip.

"It's just that I know how you react, and as much as we love Audrey," she gives her a pointed look. "We all know that she can't deal with your freak-outs on her own."

"I'm not that bad. I mean, seriously. I'm not some petulant child. So what, if I enjoy going from job to job, roommate to roommate, and guy to guy. Surely whoever you picked can't be that horrible, or you wouldn't have picked them. But it's time for the important question… Do they know not to mess with my food? I can't have another fiasco like that last steady roommate I had. She totally threw out all my takeout leftovers, and they were still slightly edible."

Audrey rolls her eyes. "Yes, we made sure he understood that. God forbid anyone throw out something that is at the point of growing stuff on top of it."

See, that's where she doesn't understand what happened. They threw out everything without even asking if any of it was still good. That's the issue I had. And let's not mention how long she'd take in the bathroom when she knew I had to get ready for work. Honestly, I never should have let her sign the lease. She was a thorn in my side from day one.

"Will y'all be there when the person you picked out comes?"

"If you want us to be," Stella shrugs. "It's one hundred percent up to you. But, the applicant is a guy. We figured that was the best option. We know how well you get along with other women… besides us."

That's interesting. It's not surprising, though. I've never gotten along with any girls, except my cousins. Maybe it's because I've grown up with them. I don't know. I just know that most women get on my nerves. Every single one I've lived with has been high maintenance, bossy, or downright awful. Like, no thank you, I already have parents. I don't need someone else telling me how to live my life. Living with a guy brings on a whole new set of issues, though. It means he's completely off limits for any kind of sexual, or romantic relationship. "Since the last guy I let stay there for a few days was a creeper, I'm totally okay with y'all being there. Especially Johnny. He can serve as intimidation."

Audrey's mouth drops open. "Wow. She's being very agreeable this morning. Who is this new version of Tiffany, and what have you done with the original?"

"Maybe we have a changeling on our hands," Johnny laughs.

It's the first thing he's said since we started this conversation, and I'm not sure how I feel about that. Is my attitude really so bad that the new guy in the family has noticed? It's not like I try to be a pain. I'm just tired of all the questions my parents pepper me with. When are you going to settle down? When are you going to have kids? It immediately gets turned to background noise because it's nobody's business but my own. I'm perfectly fine not settling down. It could happen one day, but for now, I'm good. And, I'm pretty set against having kids. Not that I don't like them, or anything like that. But I don't see myself as a mothering type. I'm too selfish and focused on me.

"Hilarious, guys," I stick my tongue out at them. "When is he supposed to come by the apartment?"

"In a couple of hours," Audrey says, matter of fact.

"What?" I screech. "My apartment is a disaster area. You could have warned me he was coming today."

"When else were we supposed to do it?" Stella shrugs. "Johnny and I are literally only here for twenty-four hours. We have to head back to Asheville first thing in the morning."

Ugh, I keep forgetting they have to account for travel time when they visit. "I think I liked it better when you lived here and didn't have to adult."

"Tiff," she rolls her eyes. "All I've ever done is adult, especially when it comes to making sure you're making smart decisions." She glances at Audrey and then back at me. "And, let's face it. You don't exactly have a great track record of doing that."

Ugh. She doesn't have to throw it in my face. She acts like it's a crime to live a life without a to-do list or massive goals to reach. I'm perfectly happy just the way I am. At least, I think I am. Lately, I've been feeling lost. With the trio disbanded, I don't know what to do with my life now. Stella was always there to stay on my ass.

"Do we need to come help you clean up?" Audrey asks before taking a bite of her food.

"No," I sigh. "I'll head home in a few to at least get the laundry off the sofa and coffee table. I mean, I don't want to him to get the wrong impression and think I'm this neat freak when I'm not."

Stella laughs, "Because God forbid, you put your best features forward."

"Don't be all uppity, Stella. Not everyone is an over-achiever." I hate when she gets like this. She doesn't mean anything by it, or anything. It's just who she is. I remember trying to be like her when I was younger because I idolized her. Then, right around the time I hit my teens, I realized that I needed to figure out who I was while still looking up to Stella.

"I'm not trying to be bitchy," Stella sighs. "This roommate isn't a done deal yet, and I *know* you need help to cover the rent."

She's not wrong, but I will not admit that to her. It will just be more salt in the wound. I can't imagine what my parents think every time I have to call them to borrow money. It's not like I do it on purpose, but Austin isn't exactly a cheap place to live, especially on the measly check I bring home.

"Fine," I pout. "I'll clean the place up some. It's not like I have anything better to do with my weekend."

"If it makes you feel any better, our house would be a mess if it wasn't for your cousin." Johnny comes to my defense. It's sweet how much he cares about Stella and relies on her to keep him in line. "Hell, the first night she saw the inside of my place, she fell through the floor."

"Yeah, my apartment isn't quite that bad." I reach across the table and pat his arm. "Nice try, though."

The chatter in the restaurant is getting louder. More people have come in, and that's my cue to leave. Even though it's not too early in the day, it's still early enough that I don't want to hear a million conversations. "I'm going to head out. I guess I'll see y'all in a couple of hours. Preferably before the possible roommate shows up." I throw a twenty on the table and scoot my chair out.

Rather than wait for them to say anything else, I turn and walk out of the restaurant. It may be a bratty thing to do, but I loathe cleaning, and it's the first full weekend I've had off in months. It's not how I envisioned spending my day.

~

PEOPLE THAT LIKE to clean are insane. I've been working on the spaces my possible new roommate will see since I got home. None of this is fun. Maybe I should have taken Audrey and Tiffany's offer to help me. I honestly didn't think it was this bad, but apparently I was wrong.

There's only one thing that could make this better. I grab my phone and the small Bluetooth speaker off the kitchen counter. Connecting the speaker to my phone, I pick a random playlist on *Spotify* and set both on the coffee table in the tiny living room. Music makes everything better.

I'm belting out a Taylor Swift song and shaking my ass while dusting the entertainment center when a deep laugh breaks through. "What the hell?"

Standing in my small entranceway is Johnny and my cousins. And that asshole is holding up his phone... In. My. Direction.

"Sorry, Tiff." He brings the phone down and shoves it in his pocket. "That was too great an opportunity to pass up."

I throw the dust smeared rag at him, and glare. "I swear to God, Johnny. If that video ends up on the internet or anywhere else, I will *murder* you."

Stella squeezes by her boyfriend and stands in front of him like she's going to protect him from me. Good luck, lady. "In our defense, we knocked and you didn't answer."

"So, you just barge in?" I throw my hands on my hips. "I'm not playing, Stella. If that video winds up on anyone else's phone, I will be pissed." If it had been any other song, or singer, I wouldn't have an issue with it. But nobody can know that I'm a closet *Swiftie*. I'll never live it down. It's bad enough my cousins hold it over my head.

Not that I'm too grunge and metal to like other music. I like to think of myself as eclectic. I'll listen to whatever moves me. But for them to now have video proof of me jamming to it, that's just not acceptable.

I hold my hand out toward Johnny. "Let me see your phone."

"Nice try," he laughs. "There's no way I'm giving it to you. Think of it as a bargaining chip should I ever need you to do something for me."

That's not what I was expecting him to say. What in the world could he need me to do for him that he needs something to bribe me with? That's a question for another time. "Since y'all are here, want to help me?"

"With what?" Audrey asks from behind Johnny. At least she didn't see me shaking my ass, even though I'm sure she heard my off key singing. "It looks like you've gotten most of it done."

That would a huge negative. "Why don't you come and see for yourself?"

Johnny moves out of the way so Audrey can get around him. Her and Stella approach the living room and gasp when they see the huge piles of crap on the sofa. "Where the hell did all this stuff come from?"

"My living room, obviously." I widen my arms to signify the whole room. "This is all crap I've been meaning to put away, but between work, concerts and my weekly brunch with Audrey, I haven't had time."

"You could always skip on the concerts," Audrey mutters under her breath but still loud enough for me to hear.

"Just because you don't enjoy listening to any sort of rock isn't my problem." I glare at her. "It's the only way I have to chill out now that I don't have you two to go out with me anymore."

"Last time I checked, I'm the only one who moved away," Stella pipes up.

"I'm not talking about you." I point toward Audrey and don't miss the guilty look she gives Stella. "Since you've left, Audrey does nothing with me anymore except brunch."

Stella turns toward our cousin and is about to say something but Johnny stops her. "I don't think we really have time for this. The guy is supposed to be here in ten minutes."

The three of us rush toward the couch, and scoop up armfuls of the random junk I have piled on it. I'm not sure what all I will do with this stuff, but it needs to disappear while the prospective roommate is here. "Where do you want it?" Stella grunts trying to keep it all in her hands.

"Um," I'm struggling with my own load. "Just throw it on my bed." He doesn't need to see that for any reason. This will be a roommate free zone. Hell, if I could afford it, my whole apartment would be roommate free. Alas, I need one. I should have moved in with Audrey when I came to Austin, but I wanted a space of my own.

I grab the dirty clothes basket and empty the contents on the floor. Screw trying to get it all in our arms. Picking up the trail of things we've dropped, I make my way toward the living room. "This should make things go faster."

I toss the basket on the couch, and we throw everything else in it. Knock. Knock. Knock. All of us stare at the door. There's no way it's been ten minutes. "Looks like he's here early," Johnny shrugs his shoulders. "Want me to let him in?"

"No," we yell in unison. "Let us get this out of here, and then you can answer the door." We scramble over each other trying to get all the random crap inside the basket. Most of this stuff can probably be thrown out, but I have a problem with letting things go.

Audrey and Stella straighten the blanket and pillows that decorate the sofa, and I rush down the hallway into my bedroom. Setting the basket on my bed, then sit down next to it. There has never been a point in my life that I've been nervous about meeting a potential room-mate. Maybe it's because I didn't meet them beforehand, or didn't pick from the applications myself, but I feel on edge. What if they are horrible? What if this guy puts on a nice front in front of my family, but as soon as they sign the lease become a raging asshole? I can be an asshole, too, if needed. I'd rather not go down that road, though.

I hear voices coming from the living room and know that Johnny has let my soon to be roommate in. Deep breath in, and out. *You've got this. It's no different from any other roommate you've had. You still have veto power if you don't like him.* With that in mind, I gather my resolve and stand up. I *need* this to work out. If not, I'll have to see if Audrey will have mercy on me and let me live with her. Even though that's disaster waiting to happen.

A quick glance in the mirror has me reeling back. My clothes have dust all over them, and my red hair is sticking out in all directions after falling from the bun. Oh well, if this guy will be living here, he'll have to get used to seeing me as the hot mess I am. Not that it matters, roommates are *off limits*.

I step into the hallway and listen to my cousins firing off question after question. Geez, I thought they had this part taken care of when I they told him to come look at the apartment.

The potential roommate is standing with his back to me when I enter the living room. "Oh, look, there she is now," Stella waves me over. "Tiff, this is Spencer, the guy who wants to move in."

FOUR

Spencer

THIS IS REALLY WEIRD. I'm not a hundred percent positive, but I don't think most roommate interviews include a cavalry. When the guy, Johnny, opened the door, I thought he might be my roommate, but then a tall blonde came up to him and wove her arm through his before extending me her hand and introducing herself as Stella.

There's no way I'm going to live with a couple. That's beyond weird. I was about to apologize for wasting their time and leave, but she said, "Why don't you come in and wait for our cousin?"

These two weren't the ones looking for someone to live with them. *Thank God*. I can't even describe how relieved I am.

Stella, says "Tiff." I can't help but think of the Tiffany that infiltrated my brain a few weeks ago. It would be too much of a coincidence for this to be the same person, and awkward.

I turn around and my eyes widen. It is her. *Holy shit*. What sort of gods are smiling down on me today? Except, I don't know where to go from here. She bailed without a single fucking word. "Tiffany? You're the one that needs a roommate?"

"Wait," Johnny steps between us, cutting off any eye contact I had with the girl that ran. "You know each other."

"Yes," I lean around Johnny and grin. This is too surreal. Normally I'm not so emboldened, but today is obviously not a normal day. I'm now looking at the red haired temptress that blew my mind. The one that didn't bother trying to get to know me even though I *know* we both felt a spark that night. "We met at a concert not too long ago."

Stella, and the brunette girl gasp at the exact same time. "No," Stella whispers. "That's him." She points at me not acknowledging that I can in fact hear her loud whisper.

I watch Tiffany nod without saying another word. So, she told her cousins about me. That's interesting, and unexpected. Why would she say anything about me if I was just some conquest?

The room is quiet and I swear you could hear a pin drop. Everyone is looking between us, but mine and Tiffany's focus is on each other. "This isn't a good idea," someone finally says. I think it may have been the brunette girl. Another one of Tiffany's cousins, I assume. What was her name? Oh yeah, Audrey.

Tiffany opens her mouth, about to say something, but I cut her off. "It's perfect. I kind of know her so it's not like we're strangers. She needs a roommate, and I need out of my current situation."

Now her eyes widen in shock. "Why are you looking for a roommate?" That's not a completely uncalled for question.

I cross my arms over my chest, and keep my eyes on

her. "I'm tired of living with my parents. It's time for me to branch out and get off their property."

"So that was why you wanted me to be quiet?" She slides one hand to her hip. "You didn't want to wake up your parents." She tilts her head from side to side, then says, "It makes sense, I guess." Then she points at her cousins and crooks her finger, telling them to come here. "I need to talk to y'all really quick."

They follow her into a room and I hear the door close behind them. "This must be pretty damn awkward," Johnny says before walking into the tiny kitchen. He opens the fridge and comes back with two beers.

"I thought the application said not to touch her food." He hands me one of them, and motions for me to sit on the couch with him. I'm reluctant to open it, worried I'll anger Tiffany. I'm not entirely certain how she's reacting about any of this.

"Yeah, that would be important if it wasn't my beer." He nods his head toward me. "It's okay to open it. She won't bite your head off. At least, not about this. Touch whatever takeout she brings home, and that's a different story entirely."

"Is she as unstable as her cousins are making her seem?" Maybe her cousin is right. This isn't a good idea. I can find another roommate. Or, I can continue living over the garage. I haven't actually told my family that I'm looking for another place to live. They will freak out. I'm their only child, and they want me as close as possible. They have this overwhelming need to always take care of me. Hell, they've barged through my door in the middle of the night asking if I was hungry because they saw a light on. No, it's definitely time for me to branch out. If it doesn't work here, then somewhere else. It's time for me to grow up.

"Naw," he shakes his head. "I think they worry about her more because she's the baby out of the three of them. Also, she's not exactly as put together as they are. She has a habit of doing whatever she wants and damn the repercussions."

That much I know about her. Hell, she left me in the wee hours of the morning without a word. Her bra the only proof that she was actually there. It's my own fault for getting myself in that situation in the first place. I'm the one that asked her if she wanted to get some food. Drunk Spencer tends to be a dumbass. He'll be in retirement if I end up living here.

The door opens and they file out until finally Tiffany is standing right in front of me. "As long as you're okay living here, then I'm okay with it."

Wow, could she say that with any enthusiasm at all?

HER COUSINS and the guy left. Two of them needing to get back to whatever town they live in and the other going to her own place. The stink eye the brunette gave me before walking out the door, proves how much she doesn't like me being Tiffany's roommate. For my preservation, or for her cousin, I'll never know.

I'm sitting on the couch taking the living room in. Now that the shock has worn off, I can finally *see* where I'll be living. There are a lot of dreamcatchers and astrological designs hanging on the walls. It's not over the top, but it's also not what I expected after seeing what she was like when I took her home. I figured the colors would be bright and bold with abstract designs filling the space. Looks like someone is trying to reach their inner zen no matter how much she fights it.

Instead of joining me on the couch, Tiffany sits down on the floor, opposite me. Is she that unnerved by me being here? She could have told me that she didn't want me living with her and that would have been fine. I mean, I hardly know her. "So," she says, eyes hitting every space except for the couch. "What do you do for a living? It's only fair that I ask since you already know what I do."

"I'm a programmer."

"What does that even mean? Do you make video games or something?"

"Sometimes," I shrug, leaning my elbows on my knees to see her better. My glasses slide down my nose and I lift a hand to push them back up.

"Like for *Playstation*?"

"No," I laugh. "The games I help develop are mostly apps for your phone, but I do a lot of work on websites and email systems."

Her brows furrow in confusion. "Where were all your computers when I came to your place? If you're a programmer, shouldn't you be able to afford living on your own?"

Wow, she comes out and says whatever is on her mind. "My computers are in the garage, so you wouldn't have been able to see them. But I do most of my work on two computers. The laptop and desktop I have in the corner of my room." She waves her hand, motioning for me to continue. She's persistent, that's for sure. "And, I do okay. I've never truly lived on my own before and figured I should try a roommate situation before branching out that far."

Traffic noise from outside filters into the room, and she's still not looking at me. It's doing absolutely nothing for my ego. *Was the sex that bad?*

"We're going to need some ground rules."

"Ground rules?" I move over on the couch so she has to meet my eyes, and she starts picking the polish off of her nails. Playing the shy card now that I'm questioning her.

"Yeah, rules," she points toward the kitchen. "I assume you know not to touch my food. My cousins said they mentioned it to all the applicants."

So I wasn't the only person who applied. I wonder what made her cousins pick me. "Yeah, it was written on the application, and you had to agree to it before the form would submit. What's that all about?"

"An incident with a previous roommate last year." She waves her hands in the brushing the comment away. "It doesn't matter, just don't touch my food."

"What other rules are there?"

She takes a deep breath and lets it out. "In no way, shape, or form are we to have sex while we're roommates."

I laugh but rein it in as soon as I notice she's not joking. The thought may have crossed my mind, but I'm not going to act on it. "What? Are you scared I'm too much of a temptation?" I don't know what it is about her, but she brings out a side of me I never knew existed. Verbally sparring with her is something I'm going to try to do every single day. Not like it matters, she's clearly not as into me as I thought she was that night.

"No," she snaps. "I just have a no sleeping with room-mates policy."

"How many male roommates have you had?" I'm

curious who hurt her so badly that she feels she has to voice this.

"That doesn't matter," she lifts her head high. "From what I've seen, it all leads to ruin and heartbreak, and I'm not okay with either of those scenarios."

"Fine," I agree, even if I don't want to. "Anything else?"

"Nope. I think we covered it with the food and sex talk." She stands up, signaling the end of our chat. "Oh, and don't hang out by the bathroom door while I'm in the shower."

"Do I even want to know?" It's such an odd comment to make. What kind of weirdos has she let live with her?

"Probably not. When do you want to sign the lease and move in?"

"Is tomorrow too soon?" I'm anxious to get away from my parents. Even if I can't have anything more than platonic friendship with her, it'll be nice being around her.

She grabs her phone off the coffee table and taps the screen a few times. "I get off work tomorrow at three. Be here around four-thirty so we can catch the superintendent before he leaves for the day."

"Sounds good." I stand and make my way toward the door. "I'll do my best to keep to myself." It's not what I want to do, but she's letting me live with her. The least I can do is respect her wishes.

"Good," she nods and brushes past me. She opens the door and leans against the wall. "I'll see you tomorrow."

I lean in for a hug, but sense that maybe it's not a good idea. I straighten and put my hands in my pockets. "Tomorrow it is." I turn and walk out of her apartment. I mean *our* apartment.

FIVE

Tiffany

"TIFFANY, YOUR ORDER IS UP." Dennis calls from the kitchen. "You better get it out there before our customers become angry."

I snort. "This restaurant caters to hipsters, they don't get angry."

"Whatever you say, kid."

Rolling my eyes, I grab the plates of food off the counter and place them on the tray. One day people will stop calling me "kid." I'm twenty-two and no longer a child. Now is not the time to dwell on it, though. There are people waiting on their food.

With the tray balanced on one hand, a skill that took me *forever* to learn, I weave around the tables. My phone vibrates in my back pocket, and I almost drop the tray of food. Who in the hell is calling me right now? Both Audrey and Stella should be at work, and they know I can't answer my phone while I'm working. We don't have many rules here at The Dreamcatcher, but no phones while working is a hard and fast one. They say it gives an off-putting impression. I don't blame them. My cousins and I have been to restaurants where almost all the employees have been on their phones at one point or another, and the service has always been shitty.

Finally, at the table I'm supposed to be serving, I slap a wide smile on my face. "How are y'all this afternoon?"

"We're great," one of the two women sitting at the table replies.

I pick up the plate closest to me on the tray. "Who had the grilled chicken salad?"

The woman who spoke raises her hand, and I place the plate in front of her. "And that means you have the chicken tortilla soup. Is there anything else I can get you?"

They both look at their glasses of tea and shake their heads. "We're good, thank you."

"I'll be back to check on y'all, but if you need anything, let me know."

The Dreamcatcher is slow today so I only have the one table. I'm hoping it picks up before I leave for the day. The tip money would be great so I can buy a few groceries. I make my way toward the kitchen to drop off my tray. Dennis pokes his head about the food counter. "How mad were they?"

Rolling my eyes, I set the tray on the rack. "Not at all. They were the picture of Southern politeness. I told you they wouldn't be upset."

"Yeah, yeah," he laughs. "One of these days you're going to get someone in your section that will give you a hard time."

"If you say so." I glance back toward the almost empty dining area making sure nobody else has come in. "Since it's slow can I take my break?"

"Sure thing. I'll come get you if anyone needs anything."

"Thanks." Pulling my phone from my pocket, I walk through the kitchen to the door that leads to the alley. It's not an ideal place to take my break, but I need to see who called me. I tap the screen and groan. Of course it'd be Mom that calls while I'm at work. It should relieve me she didn't blow up my phone after I didn't answer the first time.

I tap the icon and call her back. The phone rings twice before she picks up. "Hi, Mom," I blurt out before she's even said anything.

"You know you're supposed to let me say hello first, right?"

"I don't have much time. I'm on my break."

"Are you still working at that restaurant?" In the past, she's never once questioned any of the choices I've made in my entire life. She and Dad have always let me do whatever I want, and that might be why I'm in the roommate predicament I'm in now. It's a little late to start actually parenting me now.

"Yes."

"I guess I should be happy you still have a job," she sighs. "This is the longest you've ever worked in one place."

Wow, thanks for making me feel like a failure. "I like it here. The hours are great, and we're normally busy since we're downtown. The tips aren't bad, either." Why am I defending myself?

"You have enough for rent, right? Don't forget, your dad and I will not be helping you out anymore." Like I could forget. It's the only reason I *have* to find a room-mate. Maybe Dennis was right to call me "kid." I defi-nitely haven't done anything to make people think otherwise. I float from job to job and relationship to relationship, constantly combatting my parents wishes for me.

"I know. You don't have to worry about it, I've got it covered." At least, I think I do. Letting Spencer move in is not something I'm too keen on. I've never lived with someone I've slept with. It implies things will go further, and I'm not the type to give up my freedom to be with someone. No matter how hot the sex was.

"That's good, Dear." She's silent for a few moments and I know a lecture is about to happen. "I just wish you would settle down. Maybe find a nice boy to date."

"Mom, I don't want to *date* anyone. And I'm doing okay. Or, at least I will be soon."

"I am proud of you for moving off and finding your own way in the world." There's a *but* coming, I just know it. "But, there are times I wish you were more like your cousins. They have steady jobs with incomes that don't fluctuate. And Stella…"

I cut her off. "I don't want to be like them, Mom. My whole life you've given me space to make my own decisions, even though you'd compare me to them. I've appreciated that more than you'll ever know. But, their life isn't mine. I'm perfectly happy with my job and not being in a relationship with someone. I'm fine on my own."

"Tiffany," she sighs. "That's not what I—"

"You literally just asked why I wasn't more like my cousins. So, you can't say that's not what you meant. How else am I supposed to take it?" The silence on the other end of the line is deafening. I don't have time to keep going over the same old arguments. "Look, I'm doing the best that I can. And I'm doing what I need to do for me."

"I know that, sweetheart. I just want you to be happy and be able to take care of yourself."

Because clearly I haven't been doing that for the majority of my time away from home. So what if I had to get help from them a few times? It's not like I'm destitute on the street. "My break's almost up, Mom. I'll call you later. I love you, bye." Ending the call, I sag against the wall. I'm doing the smart thing by getting a roommate, but it seems like no matter what I do, I will never be enough. Things would be so much easier if they would stop treating me like a child and recognize my accomplishments. For instance, I didn't throw the phone against the wall when I hung up with my mother. That is a huge win for today.

The door to the alley opens slowly, and Dennis steps out beside me. "Your table looks like they are almost done, are you good to come back in?"

I stand up taller and push myself off the wall. "Yeah, just parental drama."

He nods in understanding. "I know I'm most likely your parents' age, but if you need anyone to vent to, the door is always open."

"Thanks, Dennis."

There's another win for today. I could have pouted, spilled my guts to Dennis, or texted my cousins complaining. But, I'm not going to. Opening the door, I walk right back into the kitchen and then out into the dining area. This is me being an adult and taking care of my responsibilities. I have customers to take care of, and more people to seat.

This afternoon will be another step in adulting when Spencer comes to sign the lease. I only hope it won't be a huge mistake.

SIX

Spencer

____

MY CAR IS full of boxes. I stayed up late last night packing up the essential stuff I'll need. Anything else I need after that, I can come back and get. I have to meet Tiffany in two hours. I still need to tell my parents I'm moving out.

I could have told them last night, but I didn't want my mom over here all day today badgering me about staying. She would try to guilt me in so many ways, and I don't have the energy to deal with it.

One more trip upstairs and I'll have everything I need. Surprisingly, Mom and Dad haven't noticed anything amiss yet. I hope to keep it that way for at least thirty more minutes. Then, I can go talk to them.

I have the last two boxes in my arms when I see Mom standing beside my car, peering through the windows. She hasn't seen me yet, and jumps when I set the boxes on the hood of my car. "Hi, Mom."

"Spencer, what's all this?" She waves her hand toward my car. "Are you finally getting rid of your comic collection and donating it? Your dad will be happy to have that chunk of the garage back."

Geez, even my parents have a problem with my nerdi-ness. It's not that I didn't know this already, but Mom has never come out and said anything outright. "Is Dad home?" I know he is. His car is in the garage, but I need something to say to her to get her focus off of my car.

"Yes, he's in the house."

"Want to come inside with me. I have something I want to tell you."

She claps her hands together and squeals. "You met a girl, didn't you? I can't wait to meet her."

That's not exactly a lie, but it's also not the truth. "Just come on crazy woman."

Mom rolls her eyes. "I'm not crazy." She can be though. She always makes a huge deal out of every little thing. I honestly blame my parents for the way I turned out.

We walk in the patio door that leads to the kitchen. Dad is standing in front of the refrigerator, door wide open, most likely looking for something to eat. "Dear," Mom announces our presence because obviously the door opening didn't. "Come to the table. Spencer has something he'd like to tell us."

My dad closes the door and turns toward the table. "What's her name?"

Jesus. Why do they think it's because of a girl? "Nobody, Dad. There isn't anyone I want to tell you about."

"Then what is it?" Mom asks while she pulls out a chair to sit in.

"I'm moving out." Mom gasps, and Dad nods his head as if he knew I'd eventually tell them this. "It's nothing against y'all. I'm just ready to be on my own. I appreciate everything you've done for me, but it's time."

"Who on earth will cook for you? Or do your laundry?

How am I going to make sure you're staying healthy and not cooped up in your room on your computer all the time?"

"Mom," I sigh, rubbing my temples. "I'm not moving that far away. Also, I've been doing my laundry for a long time. I'm also perfectly capable of cooking for myself as well as making sure I take breaks."

"This is because of some girl isn't it?" Gee, two seconds ago she was over the moon that I might have met some-one. Now the imaginary girl is the reason I'm leaving the nest.

"No. This is something I should have done a long time ago."

"When are you moving?" Dad cuts in before Mom has another chance to go on another tirade.

"Today, actually." It doesn't put them in a bind because they refused to let me pay rent. And if I gave them a date in the future, I know Mom would try to find some way to sabotage my plan.

"That's good. Do you need help with anything?"

I shake my head. "Not unless you know someone with a truck and trailer to get my bed and dresser. Otherwise, I'll rent a moving truck to grab it and a few of my computers from the garage."

Mom's face is bright red and looks like she's about to explode. Dad sets his hand on her arm, and sadness fills her eyes. Her baby boy is going out into the big bad world alone. She doesn't count the college years because I was still in the city. "Don't worry about doing that. Just send me the address and we'll bring it over."

Cringing, I shake my head. "It's okay. I'm probably not getting anything tonight. I packed the air mattress, some blankets and a pillow. I'll come get it tomorrow."

Dad gives me a knowing look. "Just make sure you bring someone to help you. It'll be a pain getting that stuff down those stairs on your own."

"I can help him," Mom pipes in. More like lock me inside the apartment and bolting it shut so I can't leave.

"We have those lunch plans tomorrow, Tamra. The reservations are already set, and we can't cancel them."

I seriously doubt that. He'll probably call while she's not paying attention to keep her out of my hair. Mom scoots out of her chair and wraps her arms around me, squeezing me tightly against her. I mouth "thank you" over her head to Dad, and he smiles. "I'm going to miss you so much. Promise you'll call."

"I'm literally less than twenty minutes away. You can't get rid of me that easily." Though, I'm not going to visit all the time. We all need to learn boundaries, and I need to know that I can make it on my own without my parents constantly interfering with my life.

I pull away from her. "I need to go. I want to make it before the office closes, and I can sign the lease."

"Fine," my mom pouts and stands next to my dad. "Call me when you get there."

Grabbing an apple from the table, I take a bite. "I will." As soon as I'm settled and probably not until later tonight. "Love you."

"We love you too, son." She comes at me again and wraps me in another fierce hug. "You take care of yourself."

"Always, Mom." I back away from her again and hurry out of the door. If I keep talking to her, I'll hit traffic and miss the timeframe Tiffany and I agreed on.

～

It's four-thirty and Tiffany isn't here. We're going to miss office hours and I'll have to go back to the apartment over the garage. I really wish I would have gotten her number yesterday. That would make this whole situation so much easier.

I feel like a creeper pacing in front of the apartment door. It won't be long until her neighbors call the cops about a strange man in the hallway making everyone uncomfortable. Rather than staying and waiting to see how long until someone reports me, I go back downstairs to the lobby area. Maybe I'll be able to catch her before she goes upstairs. While I still have a place I can stay, I'd rather not go back after giving my I need to spread my wings speech. Mom would never let me live it down.

Pulling my phone out of my pocket, I check the time. Fifteen minutes until five, Tiffany needs to get here soon. My thumb hovers over the mail app. The only other way I know to get ahold of her is through her cousin. I'm almost certain it was Stella who set up the meeting. She's not here yet, and I need to make sure she's all right. Even if I don't get to sign the lease today. She got off work over two hours ago, and anything could have happened.

Just as I scroll through my email messages the door slams open and Tiffany comes running through it. She sees me and skids to a stop. "I'm so sorry I'm late," she pants. "The new waitress didn't show up for her shift, and I didn't want to leave Dennis in a bind."

"It's okay. It's not five yet, we still have time." She rushes past me and waves at me to follow. "Who is Dennis?" Yes, she said no sex, but she didn't say that anything about a possible future relationship when we aren't roommates. I need to make sure I don't have any competition.

"He's my boss." She skids to a stop in front of a door. "Thank God. It looks like the Super is still here." She knocks and lets herself in before I hear anything from the other side.

"Hi, Mr. Sosa. I need to add someone to my lease."

Behind the desk sits an older Hispanic man, and he groans as soon as he hears Tiffany's request. "Again," he sighs. "I'm going to start charging you a double fee if this becomes a habit."

"It's not. This one will be on the lease until the end of the term and we can revisit after that."

Mr. Sosa looks at me. "Are you sure? The fee to be taken off is pretty high."

"Absolutely, sir." I need to make this guy like me so I can sign the lease and get on with the rest of my day. There are a lot of boxes that need to be brought in. "You won't have any problems out of me."

"It's not you I'm worried about," he mutters. "You realize it's ten minutes until five?" This time he's staring straight at Tiffany. "I need to find your file and get it all together for your new roommate to sign."

"Mr. Sosa," she grins. "You know darn well that my file is somewhere close by. We've been through this before."

"Yes, Tiffany, I know. Make sure this is the last time. I'd like to actually file this thing." He reaches into a drawer and pulls out a manila file folder. Tiffany wasn't kidding about it being close by.

"Mr…" Sosa says waiting for me to supply my name.

"Oh, sorry." I hold out my hand. "I'm Spencer Cain."

"Mr. Cain, as long as you're okay with being on the lease, I just need a copy of your driver's license, the make and model of your car along with the license plate number." He grabs a pen from his desk and hands it to me. "The only other thing I need is your signature."

Taking the pen, I bend over and scribble my name on the line Mr. Sosa is pointing at. Next up is my driver's license and I hand it over for him to make a copy while I fill out the information about my car. "Here you go," I slide the pen across his desk and he hands my ID back to me.

"Thank you." He walks to a cabinet on the other side of the room and pulls out a key. "Here's your key to the apartment. There's a fee if you lose it. Just ask her." He hikes his thumb toward Tiffany. "I can't count how many keys I've replaced for her."

"Hey," she throws her hands on her hips. "I still pay the fee for being a pain, don't I?"

"That you do." He glances at his watch and shakes his head. "It's after five. The two of you get out of here so I can go home to my family."

"Thanks Mr. Sosa, you're the best." As soon as we're out of the office, Tiffany's bubbly exterior deflates. "I really am sorry about being late. It's been one of those days."

"It's all good. Now that I have a key, I'll go grab some boxes out of my car."

"I can help you." This sudden helpfulness is odd. Yesterday she made it seem like me moving in would be horrible, and now she wants to help me. She must really need me to move in. That's the only reason for the attitude shift.

"You go and rest. I can move my own crap in."

"Are you sure?"

"Yes. Now go before I change my mind." I still want her, and if she spends more time than necessary with me, I'm not sure I'll be able to stick to her rules.

SEVEN

Tiffany

"WHERE THE HELL IS THAT ROBE?" I mutter under my breath. It's not hanging up in my closet. Pushing my shoes out of the way on the floor, I dig in the piles of clothes and random shit I've been collecting over the years. It's been months since I've *needed* the stupid thing. I usually walk from the bathroom to my room in nothing but my towel. That all ends now that Spencer is living right across the hallway from me.

It's weird having someone in my space again. Add in the fact that I've slept with him, and it's so much more awkward. So far, he is doing his best to stay out of my way, or, at least, that's what it seems like. I don't think I've ever seen anyone stay in their room as much as he does. It makes me wonder what exactly he's doing in there.

My phone rings and I stand up too fast, misjudging everything. My head hits the bar my clothes are hanging on, and I flail backwards into the wall, clothes slipping off hangers and landing on top of me. "Son of a bitch," I yell.

"Tiffany," Spencer's voice is not as far away as it should be. "Are you okay?"

Shit. He can't be in here. I don't have any clothes on. "Yes, I'm fine." Reaching out, I try to cover myself with as many of the fallen clothes as possible. Hopefully, he'll turn around and go back to his room.

"Are you sure? I heard a loud crash." He's definitely closer.

"Yep." Please go back to your room. I will sacrifice a night out on the town if he'll go away.

No such luck. A tall shadow fills the closet doorway. Damn it. Why can't he mind his own business?

"Oh, yeah. You look fine." He laughs until he looks down and his eyes widen. "You aren't wearing any clothes?" He acts like he hasn't seen me in all my naked glory before. I don't know if I should be offended, or not, that he's so stricken.

There's no way to make this situation any better. "Technically, I'm wearing part of my closet." I wave my arms in front of me, showing off all the clothes covering *only* the top half of my body.

His cheeks redden, and he forces his gaze up until he meets my eyes. "I'm just going to, uh, go." My bedroom door slams shortly after. Why does he have to be so gentlemanly? This could have been avoided if he would have minded his own business like he has been. Although, it is kind of sweet, I guess. *No, Tiffany. You cannot have those thoughts about your roommate.*

Shoving the pile aside, I scramble off of the floor, no longer worrying about the towel that was once wrapped around me. There's no chance of him coming back in here.

Stomping to my dresser, I grab a pair of panties, yoga pants, and a t-shirt. Buying a robe is now at the top of my list. This is why I don't do well with roommates. I can't do whatever I want whenever I want. And I have to be modest. It's even worse when it's someone I've had sex with.

I grab my phone off my bed, checking to see whose call caused that whole embarrassment. I guess I should be happy the bar didn't come down on top of me. Kudos to whoever built this place.

Stella's name shows up on my screen. I tap the missed call and wait for her to pick up the phone. It rings three times before going to voicemail. *Oh no, sister.* You will answer my call after what I just went through. I tap her name again and wait somewhat patiently for her to answer.

Finally, she does. "Hello."

"Is there a reason you called?" I flop on my bed, causing my purse to fall and all the contents to spill onto the floor. Today just keeps getting better and better.

"Wow," she huffs. "Someone woke up on the bitchy side of the bed today."

"You cannot imagine how horrible this day has started out."

"I take it things aren't going well with Spencer living there."

I throw my arm over my face, covering my eyes. Maybe if they are closed, I can pretend it was all a bad dream and I'll wake up. "Until about five minutes ago it's been manageable."

"Uh-oh," she giggles. "Did he try to make a move on you? You know, pick up where things left off when you scurried from his bed while he was still sleeping?"

"Hey," I protest. "I never said anything about leaving before he was awake."

"Sweetie," Stella sighs. "It's kind of your M.O. You

don't do overnights. And when you do, you make every excuse possible to leave as soon as you can."

She has a point. "I don't do relationships. Especially, not with someone who is living with me."

The line is quiet and I worry we've been disconnected. It's not uncommon considering where she lives. I still cannot believe she managed to find a town smaller than the one I grew up in to make herself a home. "So, what made this day so horrible for you?"

I give her the rundown on the events that just took place and the only thing I can hear on the other side of the receiver is laughter. Not just her's, though. There's a deep chuckle, and I groan. "Please tell me you don't have me on speaker."

"Okay, I don't have you on speaker."

"Hi Tiff," Johnny's deep voice reaches my ears. "Sorry about your bad luck this morning."

"I hate you both."

"Actually, you love us." Stella laughs. "Imagine if you told Audrey. What do you think she would say?"

"Well, it wouldn't be funny to her." Not that it is to me, either. In fact, it might be the most mortifying thing that's ever happened to me, and I don't get embarrassed by much. "She'd probably lecture me on locking the bedroom door. Or, telling me how she was right about it being a bad idea."

"That's accurate," Stella laughs again. "At least she loves us enough to worry about us all the time. You remember the grief she gave me about getting involved with Johnny."

"Hey," Johnny pipes up. "Audrey loves me."

"Yeah, now," I snort. "But in the beginning she was

firmly *anti-Johnny*. I, on the other hand, pushed my lovely cousin toward you."

"Well, thanks for that." I hear a noise that sounds an awful lot like kissing on the other end of the line. I swear if they start making out while I'm on the phone, I will puke.

This is getting awkward. Stella giggles, and that's where I draw the line. "And that's my cue to get off the phone. Bye, guys." At least, I wasn't video calling her. That would have been horrible. The time on the clock pulls my attention away from my phone. Shit. I need to get dressed and get to work.

"I HEARD YOU HAVE A NEW ROOMMATE," Janie bumps into me while we're picking up orders for our tables.

I swear this girl drives me crazy. She always acts like we're best friends, but she's kind of annoying and known for being a gossip. "Oh yeah. Where did you hear that from?"

"Your cousin. She came in a day or two ago grumbling about your new roommate situation." I seriously doubt Audrey told her anything. She probably overheard her on the phone with either Stella, her parents, or my parents. Janie is only needling me for information because she wanted to be my roommate. But, if I can't stand working with her for a couple of hours every day, there is no way in hell I could live with this woman. She would want to do pedicures and all that other stuff that I typically do with my cousins. Not that it's a bad thing. I just don't mesh well with her. I haven't since they hired her. I also learned the hard way not to tell her anything that I didn't want others to know.

Now, how much do I want to tell her? "Well, for your information, I have a new roommate and things are going great." This is a total crock of bullshit and seriously over-stating how *well* things are going, but the truth is none of her business.

"That's good." She nods her head up and down as if I asked her a question. "If that ever changes, and you need a new roommate, you know where to find me." And that's why I never told her I was looking for one.

First thing I'm going to do when I go on my break is make sure I only have shifts opposite of hers. People like her are the reason I don't do well with female roommates. Too much drama and trying to one-up everyone else.

My SHIFT IS over and I am so ready to leave this place. Most days, I don't mind working here, but today has been non-stop running around to different tables, even some that weren't mine. Mix that with Janie constantly peppering me with questions about my new roommate, and I'm ready to throw in the towel. The only thing keeping me from going home is Spencer.

"It's time to get out of here, Tif." I jump at the sound of Dennis's voice, completely forgetting that he was still here.

"Dammit Dennis, you can't sneak up on me like that."

He shrugs and chuckles. "Scaring you provides me with more entertainment than it should, so I think I might keep doing it." Dennis moves around the table until we're facing each other. The soft lights giving everything in the room a spooky shadow.

I'm filling the last of the shakers on the tables. It can be a messy job, but for some reason, I enjoy doing it. "I'm happy to know that I'm here merely for your entertainment and not to keep your lovely patrons happy."

"It's time for you to go home now. There is literally nothing left that you can do to occupy your time," he repeats as he stares at me knowingly. "Is there a reason you don't want to go home?"

Normally, there wouldn't be a reason, and I'd be out of here as soon as my shift was over. Now… There is one reason I don't want to go home. And he happens to be about a foot taller than me, wears glasses, and is hotter than anybody has a right to be. "Not at all. Just doing a couple of things that needed to be done."

"And most of those things are items I can usually never get you to do." He rests a hand on my shoulder, "Go home. And if you ever need to talk about the reason behind you picking up more shifts and staying late, you can come talk to me."

"I guess I'll get out of your hair. I'm sure your wife and kiddos are missing you." Maybe I will go to a bar. It would be more preferable than going home and having to see Spencer. I make my way to the break room beside the kitchen, but pause and turn to face Dennis again. "Also, can you make sure I'm not working with Janie?"

"You got it. I'll send the new schedule to you in the morning."

"Thanks." I continue toward the break room and grab my things. If I have any luck on my side, Spencer will be asleep by the time I get home or I will be too drunk to notice.

EIGHT

Spencer

____

HOLY SHIT. I can't believe I saw her naked…again. That's not how I envisioned the week starting out. Even if I I clung to the fantasy of her maybe bending her rules and seeing where things might go between us, I never thought I'd see her gorgeous body again so soon.

For the past week, I've been holed up in my room trying to avoid her. This whole living situation is awkward as hell, and it's not too far from how I lived when I was above the garage. At least the rent was free there, and I'd occasionally get home-cooked meals. Now I'm paying rent to not leave my room. It's ridiculous.

Moving in here was obviously a bad idea. I should have bowed out when her cousin gave me the option. Instead, I was hard-headed and signed the lease. Maybe things will get better as time goes on. It's not like I can just move out. My name is on the lease for the next six months.

The only plus side is I don't have constant interruptions while I'm trying to work. A series of letters and numbers fill my computer screen, and my eyes are glazing over. This project is almost done and I couldn't be happier. The client I'm working for has been nothing but a huge pain in my ass. Every time I send him what I hope is the final product, he comes back with changes he wants to make. Or, he's changed his mind about a certain function. I love coding and creating programs that people will use, but clients like him make me want to quit and find some boring corporate job that sucks the life out of me.

I highlight a section of code to fix his latest change when the door slams shut. I jump and my fingers hit the keyboard deleting a bunch of stuff that I didn't want gone. *Son of a bitch*. Thank God this is a copy of the original or I'd be pissed. It's a lesson I learned after the fourth change he wanted.

Glancing at the clock, I do a double take. It's after one in the morning. I've been working for the past three hours without stopping. I wonder why Tiffany is coming home so late. Even when she works late at the restaurant, she's always home well before midnight. But, it's none of my business. She made it home safely and is most likely getting ready for bed, which means I can leave my room and get something to eat. You can only live on beef jerky for so long before you have to get actual food in your system.

My chair glides along the carpet as I scoot back, and I'm thankful the floors aren't wood or some other material. I don't want Tiffany to hear me moving around. Walking to the door, I open it wide enough to peek through the crack. All the lights are off, and I take that as a clear sign that she's down for the night.

Tip-toeing down the hall, I make my way toward the kitchen. *Be stealthy like a ninja.* I'm accomplishing that goal until my foot catches on something and I go tumbling to the ground. So much for being silent. "What the hell was that?" Tiffany screeches from her bedroom door. "Spencer, is that you?"

Groaning, I sit up. "Yeah," I huff. "It's me."

Slowly standing up, I reach for the wall and flip the light switch up. If this woman does not stop leaving shit on the floor, I'm going to end up breaking something. The culprit of my graceful fall is none other than Tiffany's massive bag. I pick it up by the strap and dangle it in front of me. "Does this belong to you?"

She steps out of her room, and holy shit. In nothing but a tight fitting shirt and shorts that can hardly be classified as such, she walks down the hallway toward me. "You know damn well that's mine."

I clear my throat, tamping down my lust. This girl will be the death of me. There's no way in hell I'm going to make it the entire six months with my sanity still intact. "Is there any way you can leave it somewhere else besides the floor?"

She taps her finger against her chin before reaching out and grabbing the purse out of my grasp. "I'll think about it." I open my mouth to argue, but she holds her hand up. "In my defense, I thought you were asleep, and I just dropped it on the way to my room. Old habits die hard."

"Maybe this is a habit you could try to work on before I end up breaking my neck?"

"And my cousins say I'm dramatic." She doesn't say anything else. She turns and walks back to her room. All I can do is stare. Her ass is barely covered by the tiny piece of fabric, and I don't think she realizes what kind of torture she's putting me through. I now fully understand the saying: "I hate to see her leave, but I love to watch her walk away." Because that sight, right there, will haunt my dreams for nights on end.

"How are things going with your roommate?" Mom asks. She finally called me once she realized I wouldn't be the first one to give in. It's not that I don't love my mom, I do. She just has a tendency to overstep boundaries. Even when she promises she'll be more considerate and respect my wishes, she can't seem to follow through. She would show up at my dorm unannounced all the time when I was in college. It drove me insane, and it's precisely why I haven't given her my address. I don't need her here stirring up trouble with Tiffany. Things on that front are shaky at best.

"Great," I force a smile. She can't see me, but I'm positive it makes the word sound more believable. "I'm finally settled in and getting used to living with someone."

"That's good." She's quiet for a moment. "I had extra food leftover from the casserole I made last night. I can drop it by while I'm running errands." And there it is. I knew it wouldn't be long before she tried getting the information out of me. Not. Going. To. Happen.

"How about I come over for dinner?" Maybe the offer will get her off my case, at least for a bit. "I'm all caught up with work, so I have plenty of time to come hang out with you and Dad tonight. What do ya say?" Okay, so that might have been overkill, but I can't have her showing up at all hours of the day over here. She would freak out at the state Tiffany leaves most of the apartment in. She's not exactly the best at putting shit away. Not to mention, Mom would read way too much into the fact that I live with a woman. A woman I have absolutely no relationship with.

"Really?" Her voice raises in pitch, and I pull the phone away from my ear as I start to sit up on my bed. Mom woke me up when she called because I had another late night. I've got to stop staying up to make sure Tiffany gets home okay. She's not my responsibility but I feel this need to take care of her. "What do you want me to make? You name it, and I'll cook it."

She must really miss me if she's willing to make anything I want. She only does that for special occasions and birthdays. "Hmmm," I mutter trying to figure out the most complex thing I can tell her to make so it will take her all day. If she's busy, she can't call and bug about my apartment and roommate. "Any chance you'll make lasagna?"

Most people would buy the frozen kind and call it good. Not my mom, though. She'll get all the ingredients and make it from scratch. Nothing, not even restaurants, compares to her lasagna. "Absolutely. Maybe a salad and garlic bread to go with it?"

"That sounds delicious, Mom." See, now I've given her something to do besides obsess over what I'm doing and how I'm living my life. "What time do you want me to come over?"

"I should have everything ready by six, and then maybe we can play a card game or two before you have to leave."

The last part of her statement sounds like she's unsure of what I'll say, but if it makes her happy, I'll do it. "You bet."

"Is there anything else you want me to make? Dessert? Some of your favorite dishes that I can send home with you?" So many questions all at once. She acts like I live hours away instead of twenty minutes.

"I'm running out to grab some lunch, do you want anything?" Tiffany's voice is muffled through the door, but Mom undoubtedly hears it.

"Do you have a girl over there?" Her voice accusatory.

"No, Mom. It's the TV." Hopefully Tiffany will take my silence as a refusal. It's weird enough that she's even asking. She usually goes out of her way to avoid talking to me. I wonder what changed her mind.

"Spencer?" Dammit, Tiffany. Just go. Do whatever you have planned for the day.

"There is no way you're watching a show about another person named Spencer. Are you living with a woman?" She demands an answer but I don't have the energy to give it to her.

"I have to go, Mom. I'll see you for dinner tonight." I hang up the phone before she has a chance to argue. The stupid phone rings in my hand before I have a chance to set it down. Silencing it, I throw it to the other side of the bed, and get up.

When I open my bedroom door, Tiffany is standing on the other side. Her mouth hanging wide open. "Di—" She clears her throat. "Did you want me to grab you something while I'm out?"

What the hell is she staring at? I'm not naked or anything. Not like the way I found her the other day. The only thing I'm missing is a shirt. It's much more PG than what I saw. And it's not like she hasn't seen me without a shirt before. That night she was trying her best to get it off of me as fast as possible. *Shut that shit down, Spencer. She's already made it perfectly clear that there will not be any sort of relationship with you.* Her long red hair is pulled into a messy bun on top of her head and she's wearing yoga pants with a tank top. She looks like she is ready to work out or just finished one, but I haven't seen her do any type of exercise since I've been here. Maybe she's gotten a gym membership? "No, I'm good. Thank you, though."

"No problem. Just thought I'd ask since you've been holed up in your room so much." Her eyes travel down to the waistband of my sweats and then back up to meet my gaze. Her cheeks redden and she shakes her head. "I'll just go now."

I wonder if one of her cousins said something to her. Maybe they told her to be nicer considering I'm not a huge pain in the ass. At least, I hope I'm not. It would be damn near impossible since I don't make a habit of leaving my room unless I know she's gone. She is temptation on a stick, and I don't have the willpower to constantly fight it. I close the door as soon as she turns around because I can't watch her ass walking away in those tight-fitting pants again without doing something I will regret. The only way I can resist the pull toward her is by keeping four walls and a shut door between us.

After the stress of dealing with my mom and whatever is going on with Tiffany, it's time to go back to bed. I have a few hours before I need to be at my parents' house, and I can't think of a better way to spend my time. Setting the alarm on my phone, I put it down beside my pillow and pull my comforter over my head. It doesn't take long for sleep to pull me under its spell.

WELL, that went about as well as I thought it would. My mom lost her shit when I confessed that my roommate is female. I don't understand why she's so up in arms about it. It's not like I'm sleeping with her, much to my dismay. Tiffany stays in her lane, and I stay in mine. We have privacy and I've managed to get more work than I thought possible done while living here. For once, I don't have a huge backlog of clients sending me messages wondering when their project will be completed. The apartment is dark as I walk in, and I breathe a sigh of relief. I don't have to dance around my attraction to her and can watch a movie. She wasn't home when I woke up from my nap either, though. I hope everything is okay.

I grab a beer out of the refrigerator and head to my room. Shucking off my clothes and putting some sweatpants on, I turn on the TV and wait for it to connect to the WiFi. It's been a while since I've binge watched a show and waiting up to make sure Tiffany makes it home sounds like a good excuse to start one. I search *Netflix* for *Supernatural* and settle in to watch these two brothers kick some demon ass.

I've made it five episodes into the first season and she's still not home. Part of me itches to pick up my phone and text her to make sure everything is okay. We traded numbers when I moved in just in case there was an emergency. This seems like one to me, but maybe she's hanging out with Audrey. Yeah, that's it. She'll be home soon enough, and I'll be waiting to hear the door close as soon as she comes in.

It's nearing three in the morning, and still nothing. I send her a quick text.

Spencer: Is everything okay?

Fifteen minutes later and there's still no response.

There's only one reason she wouldn't come home, and it doesn't sit well with me. All it does is give proof that the night we spent together meant absolutely nothing to her. Why am I concerning myself with her well-being if she can't even answer a simple text? No more. Staying up late ends now.

NINE

Tiffany

I TIP-TOE THROUGH THE APARTMENT, hoping Spencer is still asleep. I'm not sure why, but I don't want him to know I was out all night. My night out wasn't intentional, at all. Audrey asked if I wanted to come over to watch a movie, and since I didn't have anything else going on, I said okay. It's been a while since I've hung out with her, and I needed a break from being around Spencer so much. The additional shifts at work are doing nothing to squash my attraction to him.

Now here I am, sneaking into my own house so I don't have to explain myself to a guy I'm not even dating. He thinks I don't know that he waits up for me to get home, but I see the blue light from his laptop shut off as soon as I walk into the hallway. If I'm honest, it's sweet. And, if I did relationships, he would be the *perfect* guy for me. When did my life become so complicated? Oh, that's right… The day I agreed to let a man I've slept with move in with me. A guy that I'm still attracted to. I'm obviously a glutton for punishment.

Just a few more steps and I'll be in the safety of my

own personal space. I twist the doorknob and take a step into the room, but my foot doesn't hit the floor. Whatever I just stepped on slides and I fall to the side. My elbow hits the door before I manage to grab the knob and use it to steady myself.

"Damn it," I mutter a smidge too loud. This hurts so freaking bad. I'll never understand why someone coined the elbow as the "funny bone." There's nothing funny about the pain shooting through my arm. At least this time, I didn't fall on my ass while naked. I'm choosing to look on the bright side. Though, I wish I knew where this sudden bout of clumsiness is coming from. Stella is the one always tripping over her own feet, not me. It doesn't escape my notice that both times I've fallen, it's happen happened while I'm thinking about Spencer.

I search the floor for the culprit of my almost fall, and my gaze settles on my hairbrush. How did it end up on the floor? I could have sworn I tossed it on the bed before I left yesterday. It must have slipped off the bed when I threw it. That's the only possible way the brush could have ended up on the floor. I reach out with the arm not currently throbbing and pick it up before setting it on my bed.

Turning around, I half expect to see Spencer standing in the hallway checking to see if I'm okay. But he's not there and silence fills the apartment. My shoulders sag, and a tinge of disappointment fills me. It's a good thing, though. If he cared, he would have rushed in to make sure all was well... right? While this realization should make me happy, a pang of sadness hits me in the gut.

～

Spencer hasn't come out of his room since I've been home. At least, not that I can tell. I haven't left my room much either. Not because I'm scared of some sort of confrontation, but because I really need to clean my room. I am twenty-three years old, and do not need to have my room looking like a twelve year old girl lives here. Audrey and Stella would be proud of me. My messiness is one of their pet peeves. Actually, most of the things that I do fall on their list of pet peeves. This small thing would make them happy, and maybe I'd look like an adult in their eyes. I love them both more than anything, but sometimes they try to parent me too much. I have parents, and I don't need them treating me like I'm their child. Even if I act like it sometimes.

Cleaning my room should not take hours. Hell, it shouldn't take me that long to clean my whole apartment, yet it does. However, finally, everything is in its place. There are no longer hairbrushes littering the floor daring to trip me once again. I think I'm going to use having a roommate as a new beginning. A chance to get my shit together and grow up.

I mean, that's what my parents have been pushing me to do for the last couple of years. It's what Audrey and Stella want. And, maybe a small part of me wants that too. To finally stop being treated like the little kid pretending to be at the grown-ups table.

With a clean room and new determination, I think I've earned a snack. My steps are slow and deliberate as I walk past his room. I'm not trying to be creepy or anything, but I want Spencer to hear me. If anything, just to give me a chance to explain. Sadly, the door stays firmly shut and I continue to the refrigerator trying to mask my disappointment.

I open the refrigerator door, looking for a package of cookie dough. The jury is out on if I will actually bake the cookies or eat the dough right out of the package. I push things around, careful not to mess with any of Spencer's food. It's only fair for me to have the same rule about food that I gave him. Damn, there is no cookie dough.

Next up is the freezer. There's bound to be something in there. It hasn't been that long since I've gotten groceries. Who am I kidding? I never actually get groceries. I normally grab a bunch of stuff that looks good when I'm walking through the store, and most of it is frozen. There's no use in me buying a whole bunch of food when I can get a meal from work.

Peering into the freezer, I spot a small pint of cookie dough ice cream. That's even better than actual cookie dough. I pull it out of the freezer and pry the lid off. Tiny crystals of frost covered the top, and I debate whether it's still good or not. If it were Audrey, she would throw it out because in her eyes, it's not fresh. But, since I'm kind of in a bad mood, I ignore it and grab a spoon out of the drawer. I don't even bother putting it into a bowl and dig right in, sighing when that first delicious bite hits my tongue. I swear, I could live off of ice cream. It might be the best dessert in the universe. It holds the magical ability to take away all of your worries and it's exactly what I need right now.

I don't really want to go back to my room. Even though it's clean now, there's nothing to do in there since there's no TV. I walk the short distance to the living room, and sit on the couch after grabbing the remote. Along with my ice cream, I think I deserve a little binge-watching session.

As soon as Netflix loads, I begin scrolling through their suggestions. The only problem is nothing sounds good.

They are all love stories, comedies or look flat out ridiculous. A banner with two guys catches my attention. What is this show? It's apparently been on for a long time, and it's about two brothers fighting demons. I love anything that has monsters in it, and this sounds like the perfect fit for my mood today. I press play and get lost in the story.

I'M NOT EVEN sure how long I've been watching this show because I didn't expect to get sucked into it. Any other time I've started a new show, or even with some of the ones I'm already a fan of, I tend to lose interest halfway into one episode. This one though… It's keeping me engaged. I've even had to press yes on the judgmental "are you still watching" question. Because yes. Yes, I am still watching. I don't see me not watching anytime in the near future. I have been up for a while, and it's a good thing I have another day off from work. Otherwise, I'd be screwed waiting on my customers.

"I see you're watching my favorite show," Spencer's deep voice is louder than the Winchester brothers arguing.

"Holy crap. You scared the hell out of me." I pause the TV and turn around to glare at him. Instead, my gaze meets his bare chest. That's twice in as many days that I've been caught off guard by him shirtless.

"You're drooling," he laughs.

"Shut up." Grabbing a pillow, I toss it at his head. "Why did you sneak up on me like that?"

"Why did you sneak through the house when you got home this morning?"

So he was awake. "I wasn't sneaking," I huff. "I was

respecting your boundaries by being quiet so as not to wake you."

"Except, I was already awake." He rolls his eyes and heads toward the kitchen. "And I'm not sneaking either. I'm hungry and have to pass through the living room to get to the kitchen."

"Maybe, I should put a bell on you."

He turns around and lifts an eyebrow in question. Waiting for me to continue.

"You know, so I can hear when you're coming?"

Spencer snorts and grabs a plastic bowl out of the refrigerator. Grabbing a paper towel, he places it over the bowl and puts it in the microwave. The low hum fills the space and I'm antsy to hear what he's going to say next. "It's not my fault you walk through here and sound like a herd of cows. I feel bad for your downstairs neighbors."

"I do *not* sound like a cow." *What a jackass*. Who the hell says that to someone?

"Maybe not, but you're not exactly stealthy either."

The microwave dings and he pulls his food out. He is facing me, and I can't help admiring the defined muscles in his shoulders. Muscles that had zero problems picking me up and carrying me to his bedroom. *Don't go there, Tiffany.*

"Mind if I watch a couple of episodes with you?"

"Huh?" I shake my head, clearing all the indecent thoughts I'm having about him.

"The show? Can I watch it with you?" He scoops up the pillow on his way to the living room and sits down on the opposite end of the sofa. "It's pretty dumb for us to be watching the same thing in two different rooms."

"I didn't realize we were watching the same thing." Or that you would intrude on my binge-watching spree and be all shirtless. The shirtless thing is going to be a problem. I can already tell. "But I guess you can watch it with me since you're already sitting down."

"You can press play now," he nods toward the TV.

I do as he's requested and pull one of the other pillows over my lap. I have no idea why except that it provides a small sense of security. The brothers on the screen are kicking ass and taking names, and I'm over here sneaking peeks at the man next to me. I'm not entirely sure what's going on in the show anymore. He's distracting me... Yet again. Pausing the show, I turn to his confused face. "Okay, we need to add another rule."

"And what would that be?" He sets his bowl on the coffee table. I'm not sure what he's eating, but it smells delicious. Like home and love, if those things had a scent.

"You," I twirl my finger in his direction. "Need to wear a shirt when you're in the main areas of the apartment."

"Why?" He shrugs and turns back to the TV, waiting for my to press play. "It's not like I'm doing anything indecent. Lots of guys walk around without a shirt."

He has a point, and normally it wouldn't affect me, but he's another story. He gave me a night of amazing sex and then ended up living here. I can't think straight when he's clothed, much less when he's not. "It makes me uncomfortable." There. That sounds like a good enough reason.

"If you say so," he stands up.

"Where are you going?"

"To put on a shirt, like you asked." He jogs to his room. His steps are so light that I can't even hear them.

"Oh," I call into the space he left. "Thank you."

He comes back in, sitting in the same spot he was in before. "Can you turn the show back on?"

"Sure."

"One more thing," he holds up his hand. "The rule also applies to you. No more skimpy clothes when you're in here." He waves his hands up and down in my direction. "It's distracting."

Maybe he does think of me as more than just his roommate. "That's fair." I nod my head, point the remote toward the TV and press play.

We watch a few more episodes, but my mind isn't solely on the images filling up the TV screen. I'm still glancing at him, longing for him to scoot closer. To pull me onto his lap. Hell, to touch me tenderly, the way he did before. But, he doesn't do any of that. His eyes are glued to *Supernatural*, acting as if I'm not there. As if he can't feel the tension building between us.

I can't take it anymore. I throw the pillow covering my legs to the side and stand up. There's no way in hell I'm the only one feeling this way. He looks up at me. "Where are you going?"

I toss the remote on the sofa next to him and turn to walk around the couch. "I'm going to bed." It's a lie. I'm not going to bed. At least, not yet. I'm going to take a cold ass shower so I can wipe all lustful thoughts of Spencer out of my mind. "Just turn the TV off when you're done."

It's a statement and there's no room for argument, even if he looks like he wants to. I stomp to my room, grab the robe I bought from the rack beside my door and march straight into the bathroom. There's only one way to squash these insane feelings. I *need* to go on a date. To see another male besides Spencer. There's a guy I know that is totally okay with casual dates and doesn't always want to hook up. Maybe I'll give him a call.

TEN

Spencer

THE CASSEROLE my mom sent home with me yesterday
smells amazing. She still doesn't think I should live with a
woman, but she's not giving me hell about it anymore.
Small victories always feel like major ones when it comes
to her. I'm hoping the homemade dinner will be an olive
branch for Tiffany after the way she stormed out of the
living room the other night.

I didn't even do anything that I know of. Though, I
am sure the blame will somehow be placed on me.
Besides, there's only one reason she would come up with
the new rule. She's attracted to me and is fighting it. Of
course, I don't want her to feel uncomfortable, so I
obliged. But it threw my resolve to be done with her
right out of the window. I'm still wondering where she
was that night she didn't come home, except it's not
really my place to question it. It's not like we are a
couple. We're barely even friends. Watching TV together
was the most time we've spent in the same space since
I've moved in. It was nice, and even better that she was
into a show I love. I've been watching it since it first

started airing and watched it many times since then. Walking in on her so absorbed in the show and seeing Sam on the screen with his research and general "good guy" vibe gives me hope that there is someone out there for me. That I can be totally badass and have a sweet side. I just need Tiffany to realize that. To throw whatever fears she has out the window and take a chance on me.

The timer on the oven beeps and I pull out the casserole. If this doesn't make her open up, I don't know what will. She seems to like food, and there's nothing better than homemade. It'll be a wonder if I don't eat it all myself. The only downside to not living above the garage anymore is no more daily meals from my mom. Even if she drove me nuts always coming into my tiny apartment without knocking, she makes the best food.

Footsteps come down the hallway, and I can't help but wonder if it's because Tiffany smelled dinner. I've noticed she rarely cooks anything that's not frozen. I'm not much better, but I do occasionally cook actual food with nutrients. "Hey, Tiffany," I call out while putting the towels back in the drawer. "I've got plenty of food if you —" Tiffany is standing at the edge of the kitchen in a short black dress, and heels that make her almost as tall as me. "Where are you going?"

"Not that it's any of your business, but I'm going out."

"With your cousin?" Please be going out with Audrey. It's a long shot hoping for that. I can tell by the look on her face, she's determined to go out tonight despite how badly I want her to stay in.

"Nooo," she draws out. "With a *friend*." I don't like how she said a friend, implying that it's someone who is most definitely more than that.

"Oh," I work to keep the rejection out of my voice. "I was going to see if you wanted to eat dinner with me."

"Sorry," she winces. "Maybe we can raincheck for lunch tomorrow? I work from two until close, so I am available."

"Sure," I sigh. This is what I get for trying to be nice. Trying to at least be friends with the woman I want more than friendship with. I grab a spoon and scoop a small portion into a bowl. "That works."

"Okay," she pauses to see if I'm going to say anything else to her. "I'm going to head out."

"Have fun on your date," I call to her retreating form.

She doesn't respond and seconds later I hear the door open then close. Looking at my bowl, I decide I'm no longer hungry. Jealousy curls throughout my body and I want nothing more than to throw the bowl across the room for letting her get into my head. I'm so stupid thinking she's interested in me. She may play coy and awkward around me, but that's not at all what she's proving to be tonight. I feel like I am back to being the kid that wasn't asked to dance at a party.

A distraction is what I need. I could go out and see if one of my friends wants to get together, but they all have lives and girlfriends. I'm lacking both. *Netflix* will have to do. I refuse to hide away in my room, though. I live here too, and I will watch TV in the living room like a sane person.

I grab the remote off the table, and lie down on the couch, my feet almost hanging over the edge. I don't think this thing is full size, and I pull my knees up until my feet hit the bottom of the armrest. The TV comes to life and I scroll through the apps until I land on the red square.

Suggestions for her account pop up, and I groan. Rom-

Com. Chick flick. Horror. Well, that last one is a surprise. I didn't picture her as a slasher movie fan. I keep scrolling through all the shows and movies that come up, but nothing is catching my attention. And, I'm sure as hell not watching anything related to love or clandestine events. Tonight was supposed to be what spurred a blooming relationship, or at least provided a stepping stone toward that, with Tiffany. The plan blew up in my face like everything else.

The only thing that might pull me out of this ridiculous funk is Sam and Dean Winchester. If they can't do it, then there is no hope for me.

Twenty minutes into this episode and I can't focus. My mind keeps wandering to Tiffany and her *date*. Is he touching her? Running his fingertips over her smooth legs. Pulling the tiny straps of her dress down. *Fuck*. I shouldn't let my thoughts drift in that direction. All it will do is piss me off. But I can't help it. She would rather enjoy the company of some guy, I'm sure she just met, than me. We live together and can't seem to spend more than ten minutes in the same room without arguing.

Pulling my phone out of my pocket, I hold it up, almost dropping it on my face. I know we exchanged numbers for emergency use only, but I think this qualifies as one. Even if it's only for my sanity and to keep my jealousy in check. It is better than what I really want to do, which is pop into every restaurant and bar she might go to until I find her. I don't know how to deal with these feelings. I've never been so enthralled with a woman that they occupy most of my waking thoughts. Hell, she's even found her way into my dreams.

My finger hovers over her name, debating whether I should text her. I don't have any right to do it, we're nothing to each other…besides roommates. I can't stop myself though. I click her name and my fingertips fly over the small keyboard.

Spencer: Are you having fun?

No response even though I can see that she read it. If she's taking the time out to look at her phone, she must be bored. Or maybe she only opened it because she thought it was an actual emergency and not me trying to pester her.

Spencer: Where did he take you? What did you order?
Spencer: Is he at least a good conversationalist?

Still nothing. What will it take for her to respond? I take a deep breath and let it out. This is ridiculous and the type of crap that teenagers pull when envy gets the best of them. A part of me is ashamed that I'm blowing up her phone. It's not enough to keep me from sending another text.

Spencer: Is he holding your hand?
Tiffany: Spencer, please stop.
Spencer: Are you coming home tonight? Or are you going home with him?

There's no response. *Damn it.* I went too far. I take my glasses off and groan into my hands. I'm a fucking idiot. I should have never text her. I'm sure I've ruined her date, not that I care that much, but she's going to be *pissed* when she gets home. There's no doubt in my mind that she's going to go talk to the leasing office to see what she can do to get me out of the apartment. I can't let that happen.

Living here has been torture with her right across the hall, but I don't want to go back to living in the tiny space above my parents's garage. How lame is it that a guy in his mid-twenties can't seem to get his shit together?

Maybe there's a way I can play it off as a joke. I don't see how, but I need to figure something out. I can't have the woman I'm living with angry at me and making the whole situation worse. The show is still playing in the background, except the only thing I can focus on is the phone sitting on my stomach. Willing it to ring or alert me with a new text. Anything to show what sort of mood she's in right now. I need to be prepared for when she gets home. *If* she comes home.

I'm not sure how much time has gone by, but the front door slams open. I push my glasses back onto my face and stand up. I should have stayed silent on the couch.

Tiffany is staring at me and has fire in her eyes. "Who the hell do you think you are?" When I don't answer she continues, "Seriously, what is your problem? You said you would be okay living here knowing that the night we spent together was just that. One. Night."

She's stalking toward me. A predator about to pounce on her prey. I've seriously screwed up. "I'm sorry. I didn't mean—"

Tiffany cuts me off, "You didn't mean what? To ruin my date? To pry information that's none of your damn business?"

I have no escape. She's blocking the way to both the front door and my bedroom. "You're right. I shouldn't have asked."

She's within a foot of me, and she pokes her finger into my chest. "You have no right to question what I'm doing. Or whom I'm doing it with. We are roommates, nothing more. Yes, we slept together, one time, but that doesn't mean you can question me like I'm some sort of criminal." Another poke. "There are boundaries that you should never cross. Things you shouldn't ask—"

I close the distance between us, pull her to me, and crash my mouth into hers. It may get me slapped, but I don't care. This is either the smartest or dumbest idea I've ever had. I guess I'll find out soon enough.

ELEVEN

Tiffany

IS THIS ACTUALLY HAPPENING? This fool thinks kissing me will lessen how pissed I am. I pull back from him and step out of his arms. "Are you insane?"

He doesn't say anything. At. All. A boyish grin lifts his lips and his cheeks are a bright red. I guess he wasn't planning that after all. My fingertips brush across my lips. I can't believe he did that. He has the audacity to kiss me after the stunt he just pulled while I was out on a freaking date. Seriously, who *does* that? He takes a step toward me and I take a step back. Warmth floods my body. Even though I'm not happy with how he acted tonight, I can't deny the way he makes me feel. There is a pull I feel toward this man who is still practically a stranger even after living with me for a few weeks. He reaches a hand out toward me, waiting to see what I will do. I could turn around and go to my room, end this dumpster fire before it begins. Or… I can give in to the lust, to the thought of his hands all over me once again. He is an itch I can't scratch, and he's provided the perfect opportunity to soothe the feeling. One more chance to be with him and get him out of my system.

There is so much hope in his eyes I'll let that one wall down and let him in. I have no choice but to let him have me after dancing around each other all this time. Not when he makes his insecurities fall away and shows me exactly what he wants from me. Instead of turning toward safety, the smart decision. I close the gap, wrap my arms around his neck and stand on my tiptoes until my lips meet his.

My body heats as his tongue intertwines with mine. His hands trailing down my sides until they wrap around me, grabbing my ass and bringing my body even closer to his. The only thing separating us is our clothes. Well, his clothes since my dress is so short it covers less than my pajamas.

He pulls back for a second and mutters, "Thank God" before kissing my neck. It's a good thing I wore my hair up. The feel of his lips working their way up my neck to my earlobe has me trembling with anticipation. He shouldn't be allowed to do the same thing to me. To make me feel pleasure with that one tiny nibble.

I back up toward the hallway, and he pulls away. "Where are we going?" He whispers, afraid to break the mood.

"My room." This is new territory for me. I don't bring guys home. *Ever.* It's a little more awkward considering he lives with me, but my room has always been off limits to everyone except me. Call it self-preservation. I don't care. It helps to keep those looking for more than what I can offer away from me. Hell, most of the guys I have been with rarely know where I live.

He nods and lifts me up enough that my feet are no

longer touching the ground. His mouth is trailing every inch of bare skin as he walks me backward to my room, being careful to keep us from running into any walls.

Reaching my hand behind me, I feel for the doorknob when we get to my room and we fall into the room. Even though I just cleaned it yesterday, my bed is riddled with clothes from tonight's date. He peers over my shoulder at the mess and laughs. "Maybe my room would have been a better choice."

"Shut up." I turn and gather as many clothes as I can and toss them on the floor. He grabs another pile and sets them on the dresser, taking more care of my belongings than I am. I take advantage and start to pull my dress over my head, but he stops me.

I fully expect him to pounce on me in the same hurried, frantic motions that just took place. But, he doesn't. He takes a step back from me, eyes trailing my body. "I didn't get to say this before because it wasn't for me, but you are fucking beautiful tonight."

My heart warms and heat pools at my center. Never has a man called me beautiful. Hot, yes. I was even called bangable by one of douchebags I've crawled into bed with. I didn't mind then because I was after one thing, a night with zero strings and full of fun times. With Spencer, it's different. It's *more*.

"Thank you." It sounds stupid as it comes out of my mouth, but I can't take the words back now.

Even though I see desire written all over his face, his eyes don't leave mine. "I'm serious. You. Are. Beautiful." I rush toward him, eager to speed up whatever he's trying to accomplish and lure him into my bed. But, he holds his hand out. "Let me just enjoy the view for a minute."

This man will ruin me. Never has anyone slowed

things down so they can admire me. I mean, I don't think I'm hideous or anything. I'm just not used to the care and tenderness that Spencer is doling out like its candy.

"Um, okay." I feel awkward just standing here. What am I supposed to do with my hands? Cross them in front of me? Wrap them around my waist? This is uncharted territory for me. By this time, I'm usually between the sheets with my date. His intense gaze would be creepy if I didn't see the adoration on his face. He is in awe, and I wish I knew what it is about me that makes him think I'm something special. I'm still fully clothed, and nobody has ever looked at me like that unless I'm as naked as the day I came into this world.

The only thing I've done is push him away any chance I can. But this, tonight, will change everything, whether or not I want it to.

Spencer stalks toward me, done with his appraisal. I step back on instinct. A game of cat and mouse, and I'm wondering when I became the prey instead of the predator.

My legs hit the edge of my bed, and I'm out of room to run. Not that I would, it's kind of nice being the one who is pursued, even if it's also scary as hell. I'm not equipped to handle anything serious. Shit, what did I get myself into when I kissed him back?

"Are you sure this is okay?" Spencer whispers into my year. Can he sense my reservations? "We can stop and it's totally fine."

Now is my chance to back down and listen to the voice saying this is *not* a good idea. That's not what happens, though. I snort, then cover my face with my hands. "Like that isn't something I've heard before, only to get the cold shoulder when I back out."

"Maybe," he kisses my jawline before continuing. "You've been with assholes before, and I'm not one. I will one hundred percent respect your wishes."

This man is a hard puzzle to figure out. How can he be so sweet, reassuring, and reserved all the time while dominating me in the bedroom? It makes me wonder how many women have seen this side of him. The thought makes me uncomfortable, and while unlikely, I hope that I'm the only one.

"Yes," I breathe out. "I want to keep going." I will make damn sure he forgets every woman before me. I want to be seared into his mind just as he has been in mine.

His fingers trail up my arms until they reach the tiny straps of my dress, pulling them down until the dress falls to the floor. I feel exposed even though I'm still wearing a bra and panties. My breath hitches as he runs his finger over my nipple. The lace of my bra providing the perfect friction.

I reach my hands behind me to take the stupid bra off so we can touch, skin to skin, but he stops me. Hands brushing against my ribcage, they wrap around me until I feel his fingers at the clasp. Within seconds my bra is undone, and he's pulling it off of me. "You know, I don't think I've ever managed to get my bra off that fast."

"What can I say? I'm a fast learner." His voice is gruff, as if he can barely contain his lust. I sit on the edge of the bed before lying back, scooting myself toward the center until my feet are hanging over the edge, watching as he strips each piece of clothing he has on, until he's as naked as I am. "I guess that's a good thing. Want to show me just how good?"

He doesn't answer me, and before long my panties are

being pulled down my legs and tossed over his shoulders. I reach down to pull my heels off, and he stops me, once again. "Leave them on." This shy guy that has kept to himself since he's moved in is giving me orders, and a thrill hums through my body. Who knew this man could shut me up with one simple sentence. The last time I was in a bed with him, I took control. Tonight… I want him to lead. To show me how much he wants me with no input from me.

He parts my legs and kisses his way up my calf all the way to my thigh before his mouth closes over my clit. My body jerks, relishing the way his tongue moves, bringing me closer and closer to an orgasm. This is going too fast. I'm going to come before he's even had a chance to be inside of me. I try to pull away from him and ease some of the sweet torture. But he grips my thighs, bringing me even closer. He doesn't let go until a moan escapes my lips and I come. Riding the waves of ecstasy, before he pulls away and climbs over me. I don't hesitate. I pull him on top of me, wanting to fill me up in the best way possible, but he leans back and jumps off the bed. He grabs the sweatpants he had on and groans in frustration. "Is something wrong?"

"I, um," he scratches the back of his head, "don't have a condom."

Rolling over, I reach to open the nightstand drawer and pull one out. Just because he's the first man I've ever brought to my bed doesn't mean I'm not prepared. "Here," I toss it to the end of the bed.

He wastes no time opening the packet and slipping it on. My eyes widen at how hard he is, proof of how much he wants me. Before I can say anything, he's over me again. Lowering himself and sliding in. Filling me to my core. He rocks into me slowly, building up the momentum and savoring every second. He's not rushing it the way I did that first night we were together. He's taking his time, kissing along my neck with each thrust.

I lean up and crash my mouth to his, tasting myself on his tongue and it turns me on even more. Spencer picks up speed, and soon he's coming. Each pulse sending me further over the edge, until I follow him. He falls onto his elbows and rests his forehead on my chest.

"That was…"

"Amazing," I finish for him. And it was. I've never felt that connected to someone during sex in my life. I've never even kissed a man after he's gone down on me. Spencer brings out something inside of me I have been terrified to set free.

He looks up and holds one of his hands in the air. "High five."

Wait, what? "High five?"

"Yep," he pops the *p*. "I mean, it was pretty awesome and most people high five after they do something they are satisfied with."

"You are so weird." I don't argue though. I'm more than satisfied, and if he wants my to slap his hand, I'll do it. My hand hits his, and he clasps it instead of letting it go. He kisses my knuckles and slides out of me.

"I'll be right back." He walks out of the room and into the bathroom, I think.

I slap my hand to my forehead and exhale. What happens now? Will he go to his room and act like nothing happened tomorrow? Pulling the comforter and sheets down, I slide between them, waiting to see if he'll come back. My eyes close, and sleep is just out of reach when I feel the bed dip behind me. He wraps an arm around me and pulls me to him, my head nestled right beneath his.

I'm relieved that he came back but also scared of what this might lead to. What does this mean for our living arrangement? That's something I can worry about tomorrow. For now, I snuggle into him and let go of the worries, at least for tonight.

TWELVE

Spencer

THE LIGHT COMING in from the window wakes me up, and I squint my eyes to adjust to the sudden brightness. Looking around, I see the clothes scattered all around the room and remember I'm not in my bed.

A grin overtakes my face as I remember last night. The way Tiffany looked up into my eyes and opened up to me. The look on her face when I kissed her to shut her up and when she kissed me back. I thought for sure she would slap me, but she surprised me instead.

I roll over, wanting to glimpse her before I go to my room to get dressed. Except… She's not there. Damn it, not this again. Just when I think she's going to let me in. Let me see beneath her snarky comments and "don't need anyone" attitude, she does this, *again*. Am I really that bad in bed that she has to sneak off? She wasn't complaining last night when I made her moan my name. Maybe I was too caught up in the moment to notice that she wasn't feeling it the way I was.

The only difference between now and last time is that

I'm in *her* bed, and we live in the same damn apartment. She won't be able to hide by running away. Tiffany will have to face me at some point. I shouldn't leave it up to her though. Hell, I'll be lucky if she hasn't already run off to her cousin's place to keep from seeing me. It's not a far stretch. The apartment is still and silent. It doesn't sound like anyone else is here, and my heart drops. One day, I'll stop being stupid and realize that she wants nothing more from me.

No, Spencer. No more wallowing in pity. I slide out from beneath the sheets and search for my boxers on the opposite side of the room to put them on before walking into the hallway. I have two options. I can go to my room and act like last night didn't happen. Act as if I don't have actual feelings for this woman. Or, I can walk my ass into the living room and see if she's there. Hiding behind my bedroom door is cowardly. I moved in here so I could grow up and learn how to handle things on my own. That includes figuring out what the hell is going on with me and Tiffany. It's time to find out how she feels about me once and for all. No more of this hot and cold business.

I'm so focused on my thoughts when I round the corner at the end of the hall I run straight into Tiffany. Hot liquid splashes out of the cups she was apparently holding and hits my legs. "Damn it," I yell and hop around thinking that will actually do anything to help.

"I'm so sorry." Tiffany sets the cups on the floor and turns back toward the kitchen, grabbing one of the few hand towels. "I was just bringing us some coffee. I was trying to make it back to the room before you woke up."

Well, that makes me feel marginally better. She wasn't running this time. Then guilt slams into me for thinking the worst of her. I should have known better. Not because she's given me any reason to trust her reactions, but because this is technically her place and I'd be the one that would have to find a new place to stay.

"Um, thanks." I hold out my hand expecting her to give me the towel so I can wipe the coffee off my legs, but she doesn't. Tiffany gets on her knees and pats my legs with the cloth, cleaning up the mess we've both made. "You don't have to do that," I bend down and pull the towel from her hands. "I'm perfectly capable of cleaning myself up."

"I know, but I feel bad." She grabs both mugs and carries them back to the kitchen. "I was trying to do something sweet and screwed it up." She looks at me over her shoulder and shakes her head. "You'd think I didn't carry multiple things in my hands on a day-to-day basis while at work."

"In your defense, you weren't expecting me to bowl you over while you were carrying them."

"Thanks," she sweeps her hair out of her face. "I'm so out of my comfort zone here. I've never stayed the night with anyone. Definitely not in my own bed."

"Never?" I find that hard to believe. She was out all night just a couple of weeks ago. "What about the other night?"

"Nope. I was at Audrey's. I passed out on her couch while watching movies." Well, that makes me feel so much better. I thought for sure she was out with some guy. Not that it would have been any of my business. It's still not, but I'm hoping that changes now. She scrunches her eyebrows together. "Why?"

Shit. She wasn't supposed to pick up on the fact that I noticed. "I was just wondering. I didn't hear you come in before I went to bed."

"I see," she rolls her eyes. She's definitely not convinced. Oh well, there's no use poking the bear, especially not this early in the morning.

"I'll make us new cups of coffee," I grab the mugs off the counter and pour the remnants in the sink. "You go back to bed."

"I can do it. Besides," she waves her hands up and down my body. "You are breaking one of the rules."

"I didn't think that one would apply after last night."

Tiffany sighs, "I guess you're right. But at least put some pants on while the coffee is brewing. You don't want to have another mishap and the coffee splash you anywhere important."

"Like where?" I'm loving her playful banter. I usually get attitude, or pretend disinterest, from her. I could get used to this new side of her.

"I think you know the answer to that." She turns and walks toward the hallway.

"But I want to hear you say it," I call to her retreating form.

"Put some pants on." She doesn't look back and continues down the hall to her room.

I'm not even sure who I am anymore. Never in a million years would I have thought I'd be making slightly dirty jokes. Hell, I had to be almost drunk to even talk to her the night I knocked her down at the concert. But here I am, owning my confidence and not letting my brain get in the way. She's right though, I need to put on some pants. Knowing my luck so far today, I'd spill coffee all over my junk and end up in the emergency room. We can't have that. Not when I fully intend on seeing what we are after last night. Where *she* stands on us. I'm sure she knows my feelings by now, but I need her to be honest with herself about her own emotions.

"WHAT DO YOU WANT TO WATCH?" We're on the couch and Tiffany is leaning against my chest. This feels *right*. Like she was meant to be in my arms. I just need to make sure she stays there and doesn't freak out about being more than roommates. I'd like it to be an actual relationship, but I know she needs to figure herself out before she makes that commitment. And I'll respect that. Some people need baby steps and don't jump in one hundred percent like me. Not that I've had a ton of experience in this realm. There aren't many girls ready to jump into something serious with a guy that until recently still had comic posters covering his wall.

"I don't care," Tiffany says. "Anything besides romance. Those are reserved for when I hang out with Audrey."

"Why do you only watch them with her?" I thought most girls like chick flicks, but apparently, I've been wrong my entire life. Or, I've just spent way too much time with my mom watching them. I've probably seen more than Tiffany has.

"Because it's my payment for when she has horror movie marathons with me." She nestles further into me. "She doesn't like them, and Stella and I love them. She sits through them with a blanket over her face for most of the movie."

"You sound like you do a lot with your cousins." This is entirely new for me, my parents were only children, and I'm an only child. Though hearing about big families is kind of weird, it is also fascinating because I have always wanted one.

"We're best friends. And they make sure my ass stays in line no matter how much I fight them on it." She grabs the remote out of my hands and finds some obscure horror film that I've never heard of. If I'm being honest, I'm not a huge fan of all the blood and guts. *Supernatural* is the only show other than superhero ones that I've been able to get into. They may fight monsters, but there is so much humor mixed in with it.

"I'm guessing you're the baby of the family."

"You'd be correct," she sighs. "It's a blessing and a curse. I get away with so much stuff, but they also have a tendency to parent me when they think I'm doing something wrong. It's annoying, but I know they mean well."

"It must be nice."

"You don't have any siblings?"

"Nope. I'm an only child of two only children. I had no one to play with growing up besides the few kids from school that I hung out with."

"That sounds boring." She sits up and faces me. "My cousins and I did everything we could together. Even though most of the time I felt like was just following them around."

"Well, I'm glad you had them." I pull her back toward me, keeping my arms wrapped around her. If she had any fears about things being weird between us after having sex, they were unwarranted. This is the longest we've gotten along since I've lived here. Now may not be the best time to ask, but I'm going to do it, anyway. "So, what happens now?"

She pauses the movie, "What do you mean?"

"With us. Are you going to say this is a fluke and will

never work?" I tighten my hold on her to prevent her from avoiding the conversation. There's no way she's getting out of this. We *need* to have this discussion.

"I don't know," Tiffany squirms in my arms. "I don't exactly have the best track record with relationships."

"Have you ever actually tried to have one?"

"No, and I never planned on it." She gives up trying to fight her way out of my arms and crosses her arms against her chest.

"Does that mean there's no chance for anything past this with us?" Her adamant refusal against relationship is a punch to the gut.

She silent for so long that I don't think she'll answer. She takes a deep breath and lets it out slowly. "I wouldn't be opposed to it, if it's with you." Bending her head back she looks at me. "You're different than anyone I've ever been with. I'm not just a piece of ass with you."

Well, that's good to know. I'm not sure what it says about me that I'm ranked right above douchebags she's gone out with. "Soooo, you're saying you'll give us a shot." I don't form it as a question on purpose.

Her head falls back on my chest. "Yes, I'll see where things go. But I'm not making any promises."

"I'm not asking you for any."

"And if things get too heavy, or begin being more than I can handle, I think we should put the brakes on the whole thing." She waves her hand around the apartment. "If things go South, we still have to live together. I'd like to do that as friends rather than enemies."

"Because we've been so cordial to each other this whole time."

She smacks my arm. "Shut up. It could be worse. We

could be at each other's throats like I was with my last roommate."

"Yeah, let's be happy for that." She snuggles further into me, and presses play on the movie. I don't even care that we're watching a shitty horror movie. I've succeeded and have the girl. I only hope it stays that way.

THIRTEEN

Tiffany

WAKING up next to Spencer is strange and satisfying. I'm
not even sure how that makes sense, but it does. He makes
me feel better than I do on my own. Not because I feel like
I need a man. I think the way I've handled relationships
prior to this is a testament to that. It is that he's comfortable to talk to and doesn't judge me or scold me. I have
enough of that with Stella and Audrey. For now, we'll see
how this goes. I've never been with one person more than
a couple of weeks, and even then I wasn't exclusive.

"Where are you going?" Spencer mumbles into the
pillow as I slide out of bed.

"This little thing I like to call a job," I laugh. "Not all of
us are lucky enough to work from home."

"Or, you can call in sick and stay in bed with me all
day." He reaches out for me, trying to grab the bottom of
my shirt and pull be back into his arms.

I twist to avoid his grasping hands. "I also have to pay
rent. Unless, you're offering to pay my half."

"I could."

Yeah, we're not going down that route. We've barely

started this whole relationship thing, and there's no way in hell I will rely on him to pay my bills. I may do it with my parents but they birthed me. It's in the rules to call them for help from time to time.

"I'm good," I search through my closet for my shirt and pants. "Besides, I enjoy working there. I get to meet new people every day and it's almost always busy." I shrug my shoulders as I pull out my clothes, "Time flies and I make good tips."

"If you say so," he tosses my pillow at me and misses.

I pick it up and throw it back at him, hitting him right in the face. "Clearly, you never played sports when you were younger."

"I preferred to mess with computers and play video games."

"I can tell," I wink at him and rush to the bathroom before he can throw another pillow at me.

My shower is quick since I woke up later than I usually do when I have to work. Spencer is waiting outside the bathroom door when I open it. "That's another rule you're breaking, Mister."

He lifts one shoulder not caring. "I'm more upset that you're fully clothed. What happened to the whole robe thing?"

"I didn't want to give you any ideas, and I'm already running late." I scoot by him, careful not to touch him. "I will not be tempted by you this morning. Besides, the rule still stands," I call back as I walk into my room.

"Seriously," he pouts and follows me. "That's a dumb rule now that you're my girlfriend."

"Not really," I shake my head, which is hard to do while trying to brush it at the same time. "It's still kind of

creepy to have someone hanging around outside the bathroom door while you're showering."

"I literally just walked up to the door right as you
opened it." He points his hand at the hallway. "My room is
directly across the hall."

"If you say so," I smirk. "I guess I should consider it a
win you're at least following my *wear clothes in the main
parts of the apartment rule.*"

He nods his head up and down. "Yes, because I
thought really hard about walking out here in my boxers,
or even nothing at all."

"Jackass," I mutter under my breath. This man is so full
of himself this morning. I kind of miss the shy, quiet guy
from two days ago. That guy wouldn't have argued
with me.

"What was that?" He walks closer to me, and I can't let
him corner me. His reflection in the mirror showing how
much distance he's covering. Stalking me and getting
ready to pounce.

"Nothing," I sing-song and turn toward him. "I've
gotta go." I give him a quick peck on the cheek, grab my
bag, and rush out of the apartment. Is that what girlfriends
do when they have to leave? I don't even know, I'm not
usually around long enough for that part. We did this
whole thing ass backwards since we lived together before
we decided to see where things go. God, I hope this
doesn't blow up in my face. I cannot afford to ruin things
with yet another roommate, even if I am sleeping with this
one.

～

I SHOULD HAVE TAKEN Spencer up on his offer to stay in bed all day. Janie is working this shift, and I completely forgot. I need to mentally prepare for the days we are stuck together. Oh well, it's too late to do anything about it now. Maybe I'll be lucky and she won't try to talk my ear off between tables and getting our orders.

That was too much to hope for. She's talking nonstop as I wait for the fries to be done for my table. I don't know what she's saying. I tuned her out after two words. "Are things still going well with your roommate?"

"Huh?" Shit, she will know I wasn't listening, now.

Janie just laughs and repeats the question. "Your roommate? Are things still okay in that area?"

"It's going really well, actually." She doesn't need to know that it only started going great about forty-eight hours ago.

"That's great." She nods her head toward the food counter, "Looks like your fries are ready."

"Thanks." I pick them up and add them to the tray of food in front of me. I feel kind of bad that she's so hung up on me not asking her to be my roomie. At the same time, I did just tune her out for a couple of minutes, and I just can't live with a person who needs to talk constantly.

I deliver the order to one of the small garden tables on the patio. It's a beautiful day to eat outside, and I'm slightly envious that this couple gets to enjoy lunch together. My mind needs to put brakes on those thoughts. It is *way* too early to be fantasizing about day dates with Spencer. *Ugh.* This is why I don't do relationships, especially with guys that I actually like. I will not end up like Audrey.

After returning the tray, I clean off the tables in my section. It's been a steady day, and the small break brings me some relief. That is until Janie comes to stand beside me. "Wow. Look at that hottie that just walked through the door."

I didn't realize people still said "hottie." It's something I haven't heard, or said, since I was in junior high. It doesn't stop me from glancing toward the door. It's okay to appreciate a good-looking man even if I'm seeing someone, right? My eyes widen at the sight of Spencer standing in the doorway, searching the room. "What is he doing here?"

"I take it you know him," Janie says. "Is he one of the guys you've dated?"

Geez, does she think I'm some floozy that flits guy to guy? She's not wrong, but did she have to say it like that? "He's my roommate." I feel no need to elaborate. What I do within my own walls is my business alone.

Janie's mouth drops open, and for once in all the time we've worked together she's speechless. I may have to drop bombs like this on her all the time. The work environment would be a hell of a lot better.

Spencer spots me and makes his way toward the table I'm clearing. "There you are." He gives me a peck on the cheek and wraps me in his arms.

"What are you doing here?" I whisper louder than I intend.

Janie grins and mutters, "I'd keep him as a roommate, too," before she walks off to take care of her own tables. I roll my eyes at her back and focus on Spencer again.

"I wanted to see where you worked, and I was getting hungry." He looks around the restaurant and then back at me. "Is that okay?"

And now I feel like shit for questioning him. I suck at

this. "Yeah, it's fine." The worst girlfriend award should definitely go to me. "Sorry, Janie drives me insane."

"No worries." He sits at the table I finished cleaning as he walked in the door. "Is it cool if I sit here, or are there people ahead of me?"

"You're fine. You came in during one of our slow times." I look around my section to see if any of my tables need immediate help, but none do. I'm not sure what to do in this situation. None of the other guys I've *dated* have ever come to The Dreamcatcher before. "What do you want to eat? I can get your order in pretty quick."

He looks at me when I mention food. "Do you have a break coming up? I need to ask you something."

Oh crap. I have no idea what he's about to ask me, but I'm terrified. We literally became a thing yesterday. What the hell could he have to ask me. "Sure. Let me ask Janie if she'll watch my table."

She's waiting for me by the food counter like a lion ready to pounce. "Oh my gosh! He's your roommate and your boyfriend." She's bouncing up and down on her toes. "No wonder things are going great."

"Yes," I draw out. "Can you watch my tables while I take my break?"

"Absolutely." She looks over at the table he's sitting in. "I'll bring y'all some drinks and fries, too."

"Thanks." Maybe she's not as horrible as I've made her out to be.

I rush back to the table, and slide into the chair opposite him. "What's up?"

"What are you doing next weekend?"

"No idea," I shrug my shoulders. "I haven't gotten my work schedule, yet."

He taps his knuckles against the table, nerves getting

the best of him. I wish he would come right out and ask whatever it is he's wanting an answer to. "If your boss hasn't made the schedule, can you ask for next weekend off?"

"Why?" He seems nervous to even ask me, and I'm ninety percent sure it has to do with the fact that we are a baby couple. We haven't yet found our legs, and probably won't for a while.

He grimaces. "Here's the thing. I have tickets to Comic Con next weekend. A buddy of mine was supposed to go with me, but something came up. He's out. I really don't want to sell my tickets, but I don't want to go alone, either." He takes a deep breath. "That's where you come in. If you want to," he waves his hands toward me. "No pressure or anything. I understand if it's not something you're in to."

I bust out laughing. I can't help it. *That's* what he was so nervous to ask me? "Seriously?" Spencer's face falls, and he moves his hands from the tabletop to his lap. And now I feel like the biggest bitch that's ever lived. "Sorry. I'm not making fun of you, I swear. It's just that I was expecting some life changing question, but I definitely wasn't expecting that."

He perks up a bit at that. "Does that mean you'll go with me?"

I feel so bad that he's ashamed to like the things he does. Everyone has something they enjoy and they shouldn't have to hide it. I knew what I was getting into that first night I met him and saw the posters on his wall. I will not make him feel like shit about geeking out over comics. "Of course, I'll go. Getting off shouldn't be a problem since I work most weekends. That just means I'll have to work all week."

His shoulders sag in relief, and I hate that people have made him feel like crap because of his hobbies. I've always been a big believer in doing what you want. "He'll let you off just like that?"

"Perks of working here for a while." I lean in closer and beckon him to come closer. "Don't tell anyone, but I'm his favorite employee." I whisper. Smacking my hand on the table, "Besides, with all the extra shifts I've picked up, I deserve a weekend long break out of town. Just let me know the exact days, and I'll ask."

Janie brings over an order of fries and two sweet teas before winking at me and walking away. I'm sure I will get a million questions when Spencer leaves. He grabs a fry and dips it in ketchup. "I'm honestly surprised you said yes. I didn't think it would be something you're interested in." He pops the fry in his mouth and waits for me to say something.

"I've never been to anything like it, but I'm always up for trying new things."

"Good to know."

Now that I'm no longer freaking out over his big question, I can finish up my break and get back to work. I'm going to have to research what one wears to comic con so I can be fully prepared next weekend.

FOURTEEN

Spencer

WE MAY BE in the same city, but driving to the event venue is a pain. Traffic clogs the streets in every direction and it might have been faster walking here from the apartment. I'm just happy I got a hotel room next to the event, and Tiffany had no issues with staying there for the weekend.

"Wow," she says as she looks out the passenger side window. "You weren't playing when you said people dress up for this thing."

"It's fun for them." I spot a few people dressed up as various movie or comic characters walking down the sidewalk to the event. "A chance for them to be someone else for a day, or show their love for their favorite characters."

Tiffany turns toward me and raises her eyebrows. "Why aren't you dressed up? I know you have a couple of different characters that you love."

My cheeks redden. I've never brought a girl I was dating to one of these things. Most of them would outright laugh in my face, which is what I thought Tiffany was doing when I asked her. But, she didn't. How could she possibly understand how hard it was for me to ask her to take part in this part of my fandoms.

"I didn't want to scare you off. Most girls that aren't into comics and superheroes are put off by this sort of thing." I reach across the console and grab her hand. "I don't want to ruin things before we've even had a chance to see what happens."

"Dude," she laughs. "You've seen, or heard, how badly I fight my cousins on conforming to their idea of life. I'm a huge advocate of people doing what makes them happy. I would never belittle you for wanting to have fun doing something you love."

"Thanks." Her reassurance dulls some anxiety I had about bringing her. Knowing that she won't make fun of me, the other fans, or cosplayers will make today much easier. We pull into the valet of the hotel we're staying at and grab our bags before they take off with the car. The event is right across the street, and I'm not trying to fight to get into their parking garage. "Let's get checked in and then we can head over."

As soon as we're in our room, I put away my suitcase and get our weekend passes. "Why are there two beds instead of one?"

It's a reasonable question, but I can't help laughing inside that it's her first question. "Because I was originally sharing the room with a friend, and I'm not a huge fan of cuddling with him. You, however," I sweep her into my arms, "are a different story. I'm good with whichever bed you want to sleep in."

"We'll see how today goes," she winks at me before breaking my hold. "Let's get this show on the road. I'm ready for a new adventure."

Her love of life and living with no rules no matter how

things turn out is what drew me to her in the first place. One day, I hope I can be like this red-headed beauty, and not care what others think of me.

"HOLY SHIT," Tiffany's eyes widen when she sees the line we have to get in. "I was *not* expecting so many people."

"This is nothing," I grin. "There will be more as the day goes on. Everyone in this line is a diehard fan and love going to Cons."

She's eyeing everyone and pointing out a few people with elaborate costumes. "Can we get pictures with the people dressed up? Please, say yes. I would love to get a shot with some of them to show Audrey and Stella."

Nodding my head, I pull her closer to me. "Yep. You just have to ask them first." I try to look at the event from her eyes, someone who has never been, or even realized this world exists. "The best part is when little kids come for the first time and see their favorite superheroes in real life. It's like Christmas morning for them."

"All I'm saying is if there is a hunky Thor, it might be hard to pull me away."

"I didn't know you liked Thor." In all the time I've spent watching shows on her *Netflix* account, I've never seen a superhero movie in any of the suggestions.

"It's more that I like Chris Hemsworth dressed up as Thor, but I've seen the movies plenty of times."

"That's good to know." I'm not as muscular as Thor, but I'm sure I could find something and wear it for her. I mean, it could be fun. Or it could blow up in my face and she'll dump me on the spot. Really, it might go either way. "Are you sure you're ready for this?"

"Absolutely," she grins and looks up at me. "It's a new experience. Let's do this thing."

The doors open and the line finally speeds up. When we get to the entrance, they check our badges and bags. I learned a long time ago to bring a backpack for any purchases I make. Let's be honest. I will buy a lot of stuff I don't really need, but I have to have it because it's part of one of my fandoms. "What do you want to do first?"

Tiffany is looking at the surrounding chaos. People dressed up, posters, and lines going in every direction. "I'm not even sure what there is." She glances at a board that has the events for today listed. "It's a little overwhelming. Even the big music festivals I've been to haven't been this… much."

"We can start off with a panel until you get your bearings." The marketplace sign is to my left, and I wonder if she'd rather do that. "Or we can walk around the market hall and check out what the different shops have."

"There's shopping here?" She shrieks and jumps up and down. "Let's do that. Shopping is my other hobby besides going to concerts."

We turn into the room and run into cosplayers left and right. "Do you want to get a picture with any of them before we go any further?"

"I don't know who any of these people are supposed to be."

"It's okay. I'll explain which characters they are portraying when we get back to the room."

"Can you ask them?"

I walk over to the group and ask them if Tiffany can get a picture with them. Naturally, they all agree and she keeps talking to them after I've snapped the photos. I stand back and watch her take in this part of my life like a champ. She's asking them about the makeup and how long it takes to get ready. I love that she's not faking her excitement or interest.

"Where to next?" She loops her arm into mine and drags me toward the shop booths.

"Wherever you lead me," I laugh. I think I've lured her in. Hook, line and sinker. Hopefully, even if things don't work out between us, she'll continue to attend cons like this. She has the same sort of excitement I felt at the first one I went to.

We stop by a few booths. She's buying all sorts of fandom soaps and I have no idea how she's going to use them all. An art booth catches her eye and she pulls me to a stop. "I'm going to need a few of these for the living room. What do you think?"

The artist steps in front of us after overhearing her question. "If you like fantasy, I don't think you can go wrong with any of these. How long have you been together?"

"Two weeks," I say as I smile down at the woman who has captured my attention, and try to tamp down the fear of losing her that keeps bubbling up at unexpected times.

"Wow, and you already live together?" I feel like she's being a little judgy. Who is she to tell us how to do things? We could have known each other for years and just realized that we're perfect for each other.

"It's a long story," Tiffany laughs. "If I buy the ones I want now, can we leave them here until the end of the day?" She glances around the massive room. "I don't really want to carry around everywhere and risk damaging it."

"Absolutely," the woman beams at her. Of course she's all smiles now when she knows she's going to make a sale. Where are all your judgemental questions now?

"Thank you." Tiffany points out the ones she wants and hands the artist her card. "Spencer, can you make a note of which booth this is on your little map thingy? I don't want to forget when we come back for the art."

"You've got it," I pull the map out of my pocket and swing my backpack around to grab a pen. After the location has been marked, we continue on our way.

We're almost to the end of the marketplace area when Tiffany gasps. "Are they really doing tattoos here?"

I look around for the area she's talking about and notice the "Tattoo Zone".

"Looks like it. Why?"

"I want to get one." She's steering me toward the line of tattoo artists, checking out their work, and trying to decide where she wants to get ink.

"Are you sure?" I don't have any tattoos. The thought of needles going into my skin repeatedly weirds me out.

"Yep." She stops in front of a booth with a sign that says *Life in Ink*. "And this is the artist I want to get it from."

A man with tattoos covering his arms walks up to us. "Hi, I'm Adrian. Are you looking to get some ink today?"

"Not me." I point to Tiffany, "her."

"Yes," she screams. "I've always wanted one, and what better time than during my first time at Comic Con."

"I couldn't think of a better reason to get one." Adrian smiles at her, and I don't like it. "Soph, can you bring the schedule for the rest of the day to see when we can fit…"

"Tiffany," my girlfriend supplies.

"Tiffany in." Adrian motions for a brunette girl to come over.

"Absolutely." The brunette comes over with a piece of paper and examines it like it's a test. "It looks like we have an opening in about two hours." She looks at Tiffany, "Will y'all still be around then?"

Tiffany turns her excited gaze to me, "Will we?"

"We're here all day, weirdo." She wraps an arm around my waist and I love that she is willingly letting this tattoo artist know that she's taken.

"Alright," Soph says and writes something on the form. "My *boyfriend* here is one of the best tattoo artists in Dallas. You won't be disappointed. Just have an idea of what you want him to do when you come back."

My heart lifts when she says the word boyfriend, and I know she did it for my benefit. Somehow she saw just how uncomfortable I was with Adrian smiling at Tiffany. I have got to get this jealousy bug under control. It's bad enough that I'm awkward in my own skin. I don't need to let that overflow into my relationship.

"Awesome," Tiffany gives Soph a high five. See, people do that when they are happy about something. I'm not going to bring that up here, though. "I want to check out whatever panel is going on right now. Preferably horror themed."

Who am I to deny this woman anything?

We're about to walk into one of the large meeting rooms when she stops. "By the way, we're going to have to go by a store tonight."

"Why is that?" The hotel we're staying in has room service and almost anything we could possibly want.

"Because you and I," she points back and forth between us. "Are going as Sam and Rowena from *Super-natural*. It's a perfect fit. You're tall, nerdy, and hot as hell. And I'm the red-headed, smart ass, witch."

"Works for me." I open the door and motion for her to go ahead of me. If she didn't have me falling for her before, she does now. Never in a million years did I think I would find my match. Someone to binge watch TV shows with, go to cons, and cosplay. I feel like I've just hit the damn jackpot.

FIFTEEN

Tiffany

I CAN'T BELIEVE I got a tattoo over the weekend. Audrey is going to lose her shit when she sees it. The whole weekend was amazing, and not even Janie's mindless chatter can bring me down.

"How was your weekend?" she asks while closing up the restaurant.

I'm not even sure how to describe it. "I went to Comic Con with Spencer."

"I feel bad for you, then." She sweeps her section and bends down to push the dirt into the dustpan. "One of my ex-boyfriends thought it would be a fun date, but I would have rather watched paint dry."

That seems a little harsh. "It couldn't have been all that bad." I can't imagine anyone going and not having the time of their lives.

"It wasn't great either." She tosses what she collected in the dustpan in the trash. "I was bored out of my mind. There is nothing fun about hanging out with grown ass people playing dress up."

Whatever brownie points she had with me are going

right out the window. "Don't you do the same thing on Halloween?"

"Yeah, but that's different. These people do it all the time. Whereas, I might do it once a year."

I'm choosing not to comment on that. Why does she care what they do with their time? They aren't forcing her to hang out with them, or dress up. I was impressed with the amount of work the cosplayers put into their costumes. Everything was so detailed and looked like it belonged in a movie. I felt like a phony when Spencer and I dressed up on the second day. "Well, I think I will head out if we're done." This conversation is going downhill and I don't want to hear anymore from her.

"Yep," she heads to the kitchen. "That was the last bit that needed to be cleaned up."

"Alrighty, I'll see you on our next shift together." I walk to the break room to gather my things and let Dennis know I'm leaving. He's been doing his best to keep Janie and I off the same shifts, but it's not always possible. It will be a lot easier when we find another waitress to balance out the workload. The problem is he can't find anyone dependable. They show up for a couple of days then disappear when they realize this job isn't easy.

"I'm out of here, Dennis."

"Be careful on your way home. Do you still want extra shifts?"

A couple of weeks ago, the answer would have been a resounding yes, but now I'm enjoying my free time with Spencer. "Not really." He says nothing and I add, "unless you need me. Then I'll be here."

"You're fine. I just wanted to make sure." He straightens the stack of papers in his hands. "I'm glad everything is working out. Tell Janie to head out when you leave. I just need to finish up this paperwork and I'll be going home."

"Will do." I wave before turning toward the main area. "See you later. Don't work too hard."

"Never," he laughs. "That's what I have y'all for."

"Whatever, Old Man." I hurry down the hall to go back to the dining area. "Janie."

"Yeah," she calls from the kitchen.

"Dennis said it's time to get out of here." Despite her pissing me off with her comments about the cosplayers, I'm not a total bitch. "Have a great rest of the night."

"You too," she hollers on her way to the break room.

The sky outside the front windows is pitch black, and although the tips are better when I work evenings, I hate having to get home in the dark. I let myself out of he door, locking it once I'm outside. Janie will have to go out the back since she hasn't been here long enough to be given a key to open or close on her own.

The key is being a pain, and I don't realize that someone has come up behind me until they wrap their arms around me and I scream. Pulling the key out of the lock, I whip around to face my attacker, ready to stab. But they pull back, hands in the air. "Calm down. It's just me."

"You gave me a mini heart attack, Spencer." I slap him with the hand not holding the keys. "Don't you know you're supposed to announce yourself before you sneak up on someone?"

"That would negate the sneaking part, I think." He laughs and dodges my next hit. "Next time I'll remember to cough loudly so you know I'm here."

Dennis comes running around the corner, and skids to a stop in front of the door. Wow, for a man his age, he sure can move. He unlocks the door and throws it open. "Is everything okay? I heard screaming." I'm actually a little surprised with all the street traffic. Being downtown brings in background noise at all hours of the day.

"Yes," I sigh. "I'm fine. My bonehead boyfriend is the cause."

Spencer winces when the words leave my mouth. "Hi," he extends a hand toward Dennis. "I'm Spencer, the bonehead boyfriend."

"So you're the reason she's been more chipper than usual." Dennis grasps Spencer's outstretched hand and shakes it. "It's nice to meet you, I'm Dennis."

"And you're the reason she avoided the apartment so much when I first moved in."

Dennis holds his hands up in surrender. "I only did what I was asked. She wanted more hours, and I gave them to her."

"Understandable." Spencer puts his hands in his pockets and takes a step back. "I just came to pick her up."

"I'm happy someone is looking out for her," Dennis nods toward the guy who is slowly capturing my heart. "Someone needs to. This girl worries me sometimes."

"Hello," I wave my hands up and down. "That girl is standing right here and is perfectly capable of doing things." Frustration that they are talking about me like I'm a child fills me. This is something Stella and Audrey would do. Well, old Stella. She's mellowed out a lot since she's starting dating Johnny.

"I know you are," Dennis concedes. "I only wish you'd think things through a little more."

"Noted." Now he sounds like my parents and I'm not sure how I feel about that. "Are you ready to get out of here?" I grab Spencer's hand and pull him down the sidewalk. "I'll see you later, Dennis."

"I'll text the new schedule to you in the morning. Have a great night," he calls to our retreating backs.

Spencer bends down and whispers in my ear, "I parked in the other direction."

"Just go with it," I bite back. "We'll wait a few minutes and then turn around."

"Are you okay?"

"Yeah," I sigh. "Just annoyed with my boss. He's never once said anything like what he did to you. I know he cares, but there's a better way to go about voicing it than what he just did."

Spencer glances behind us before pulling me into his arms. "I think we're good to go. But, before we do, I want you to know that I think you're fully capable of taking care of yourself. We all make mistakes, but it's a chance for us to learn from them."

"Thanks," I mutter. "I needed to hear that."

His lips graze my forehead and everything he said feels true. I mean, I did what I thought was best when I let my cousins pick my roommate. So far that is working out better than I thought it would. We turn around, passing The Dreamcatcher once again, and get into his car parked at the end of the block.

"Let's get out of here," he grabs my hand after putting the car in drive. He merges into the traffic easily, but he misses the turn we need to take to go home.

"Where are we going?" I'm not sure I have the energy to do anything else today and my tattoo is itching. I dig through my purse for the lotion I threw in there this morning.

His gaze meets mine for the briefest moment before he focuses on the road again and smiles. "It's a surprise."

Instead of complaining about being tired, I sit back and enjoy the ride. The red taillights blurring by as we get on the highway on our way to an unknown destination. Dennis's worries still wiggle in the back of my head, but I will not focus on them. I'll talk to him when I go back into work. It's not worth ruining my mood for the rest of the night even though I wish we were heading home to snuggle up on the couch while binge watching TV.

I MUST HAVE FALLEN asleep because I open them when the car comes to a stop and Spencer puts it into park. "Rise and shine, Sleepyhead."

"Sorry," I mutter. "I didn't realize I was that tired. Was I asleep long?"

"Nope," he shakes his head. "Only about ten minutes. We're still in Austin."

"Good to know." I'm not prepared to go anywhere else. Loud music accompanies the sound of cars driving up and down the street, and my interest is piqued. "Are we at a bar?" It's been a while since I've been out. Audrey doesn't like going, and from the look of the grungy walls, this isn't a place I would normally frequent.

"Yep." He turns the car off and rushes around to open the door for me. Ever the gentleman, this one. "There is a local band playing here tonight similar to what you like. I thought since you went to Comic Con with me, I would treat you to a night of music."

"It's like you know how to read me or something." I grab his hand, letting him pull me out of the car.

"I like to think I do," he shuts the door behind me. "And it looks like you might need it today."

He has no idea. Between the crap with Janie, then Dennis's comments… I need to decompress. The only thing that has ever worked besides a night out with my cousins is music. There's a short line at the door, but we bypass it completely. "Are you special or something?"

"I know the owner," Spencer grins. "I designed the website for this bar."

"Wow, look at you," I laugh. "Any other bars you've done tech work for? It would be awesome to get out of some of those lines."

"Doubt it," he gives me a knowing look. "But I can always check." It's nice to have a boyfriend with connections. I mean, if things work out between us.

If I thought the music outside was loud, it's deafening in this small bar. The outside looks bigger than the inside, and while it would put most people off, I feel at home here. The band on stage isn't all that bad either.

The atmosphere is chaotic but cozy at the same time as if I'm on the same musical high as the band playing. These are my people. I wrap my arms around Spencer and wonder how I found a guy that gets me so completely. More than even my cousins have and I've known them my entire life.

SIXTEEN

Spencer

SEEING Tiffany completely let go of all her stresses at the concert the other night was exactly what I hoped for her. I don't know what prompted me to take her. It was just a gut feeling that she needed a pick me up. Apparently, I was right. She never told me what put her in a bad mood, but I don't think it was just her boss's comments. We're working on her opening up more. I want to break down all the walls she has put up.

A quick glance at the clock tells me I have roughly three hours to finish up this project before Tiffany gets back. The great part about working from home is I can sync my schedule with hers. Normally, I'm a night owl and do everything then. But, I've noticed I get much quicker responses when I work during the day like normal people. This should have occurred to me before, but I'm stubborn and don't like changing my routine unless I have a good reason to do it. And Tiffany is definitely a good reason.

My phone rings, and I'm hoping it's Tiffany calling during her break. Sadly, it's not. Mr. Harrison, also known as my pain in the ass client, is who shows up on the screen.

"Hello," I answer on the third ring, not wanting him to think I'm making myself too available. He'll take advantage of it.

"Spencer," he yells into the phone. "I'm glad I caught you."

"Is there something you wanted to discuss? I'm putting the finishing touches on the app you wanted for your customers." Please, don't let this be a call to change things.

"About that." Here we go. I really need to put a limit on how many changes can be made before they are charged more. "Can you change the colors again? Also, some of my employees tested out the app and they said the buttons aren't linking to the correct inventory."

I pull up the notes app on my laptop and start typing in his requests, even though I'm sure he will change his mind… again. "I can change the colors, no problem. Is the color scheme on the website changing as well? It's easier if they branded in the same style."

"Yes," he replies. "Our tech department is working on that now. What about the buttons not linking?" His voice is panicked and I'm not sure if I want to scream or sigh.

"As long as you send me the color codes, I can get those switched out." I take a deep breath and tell him the same thing I've told him time and time again. "The buttons aren't linking through because it's not live yet. When you send the information on the inventory set up, I can put those into the app and everything will work seamlessly."

"Thank goodness," he breathes right into the phone. "I

was starting to worry since the launch date for the app is looming."

This, ladies and gentlemen, is why you don't promise customers something by a certain date. When changes are made this late in the game, it's almost never going to be ready in time. "If you get me the information in the next couple of days, I'll make the changes and have it over to you for approval by the end of next week."

"You are a lifesaver, Spencer." He says something to somebody else and then continues to the conversation he is having with me. "I'll get the new information sent over as soon as possible." Then he hangs up. No goodbye, or thank you, just silence on the other end of the line. I swear Mr. Harrison is going to drive me to drink.

Now that I'm stuck waiting on his crap, I need to see what else is in the queue. There's nothing pressing though. Most of my other clients have their shit together before they even contact me. They know what they want and send it over in a nice checklist format. I wish Mr. Harrison was more like that. It would make my job a hell of a lot easier.

I'm about to close my computer down when an email pops up. It's not from the form on my website, but I recognize the name of the email. It's the band that played the other night.

Spencer,

Well, I hope this is the right Spencer. Rob showed us the website you created for him, and we would like for you to create ours. We've been using social media, but if we want to have a presence, we know we need to up our game. Hit me up with your rates and we'll talk.

-Dale

It's good to know that Rob was so impressed with my work that he referred me Crooked Halo. Now I need to figure out if I will work with Dale, or not. They are a newbie band and I'm sure they don't have what I charge for complete website builds. On the other hand, I've never created a site for a band, and it could be fun. I'll ask Tiffany what she thinks when she gets home. She can sense whether something is a good idea, and her opinion matters to me.

"WHAT'S THAT DELICIOUS SMELL?" Tiffany calls out. I've been in my room playing video games and ignoring all work responsibilities. I'll get it done. Mr. Harrison's app is the most pressing one, and he still hasn't gotten the information back to me.

I walk out of the room and down the hallway, wearing clothes per *her* rules. You'd think she'd lay off them, but nope, she's stubborn as hell. "Some casserole my mom sent home with me."

She throws her bag on the counter and wraps her arms around me. "Has your mom made all the meals you've been cooking?"

"I swear you never look in the freaking freezer." I walk her backward until I'm in front of the refrigerator and open the freezer door. "Any time I visit her she sends food with me. I can't cook for shit."

"At least you're honest about it," she laughs. "Most guys would have taken all the credit. Then one day their girlfriend, or wife, will find them unloading casserole dishes from their car and hiding them behind the ice cream."

"You realize not everyone eats ice cream, right? Some people actually use their freezers for real food."

She pulls away from me. "Last time I checked ice cream has dairy in it. And, dairy is a food group. Therefore… Ice cream is real food."

"Is this an argument I can win?"

She scrunches up her nose, looking adorable. "Probably not. Better cut your losses while you can." She looks around me at the stove. "How long until it's ready?"

"About thirty-ish minutes. Why?"

"Good, I want to get cleaned up." She pulls her shirt away from her and groans. "One of the cooks called in sick and I offered to help in the kitchen. It reminded me why I prefer giving people their food instead of cooking it. I burned at least ten things today."

"All I'm hearing is that you can't cook, either."

"Why do you think I have so much ice cream and frozen pizza? If I tried to cook something, there's a big likelihood that I would catch the whole building on fire."

"Noted." I push her toward the hallway. "Go take a shower. I'll get the plates and stuff out. It should be ready when you get out."

"Or, you could join me…" She lets the statement trail off, waiting for my response.

"Then we'd both starve. There's plenty of time for that later." I shoo her away. "Besides, I have some news, and I want to get your opinion on it."

She crosses her arms across her chest, and all it does it amplify how well-endowed she is. "You realize I have zero patience, and need to know now, right?"

"You'll have to wait."

"Ugh," she stomps her foot. Is it weird that I'm attracted to her even when she's trying to throw a tantrum? "You sound just like Stella and Audrey."

"I've been called worse. Go take a shower."

She doesn't say anything else and stomps toward the bathroom. The door slamming shut to show how much I've annoyed her.

OUR FOOD IS SEPARATED onto plates and sitting on the coffee table when Tiffany gets out of the shower. I would advocate for a kitchen table, except there's no room for one in this tiny apartment.

"So are you going to tell me the news?" She sits down and looks at the plate. "What is that?" Revulsion. It's written all over her face. "How can something that smells so good come out of the oven looking like something a cat threw up?"

"It's chicken spaghetti. It's supposed to look like that." I see what she means, but it tastes better than it looks. "You've never had it?"

"Uh, no," she shakes her head back and forth. "And I'm not sure I want to try it now."

"Just take a bite, you big baby." I twirl some noodles onto my fork and fly it through the air like an airplane. Her mouth is tightly sealed. "If you try it, I'll tell you the news."

Tiffany glares at me, but she finally opens her mouth. Her eyes close, and she makes a *mmm* sound. "Okay, so it's not that bad." She swallows and picks up her own plate and fork, digging in like she didn't insult it moments ago. "Now, tell me the news."

"Remember that band we saw the other night, Crooked Halo?" She nods while shoveling food in her mouth. It's like she hasn't eaten all day, and I wonder when they will hire more people so she's not juggling so much. "Well, they sent me an email today and want me to build them a website."

"That's fantastic," she bounces up and down on the couch, spaghetti noodles sliding to the edge of her plate. She scoops them back toward the middle and sets the plate down before another near spill happens. "You're going to do it, right?"

"I wanted to get your opinion on it before I answered."

"Hell yes! You should do it. They were fantastic and big things are coming for them. Mark my words."

"Are you sure?" I pause while she nods emphatically. "It will definitely push my boundaries. I've only ever taken on corporations, and this will be a whole new ballgame."

"Absolutely." She picks up her plate to eat again. "First thing in the morning, you better send them a response." Grabbing the remote, she pulls up the show we've been binge-watching. "But now, we watch. I need to know what happens next." I've already seen this entire series multiple times, but seeing her get into it makes me happy. We're on the episode where some heavy stuff goes down with a relationship and the character decides it's best to leave the woman he loves to protect her. I wonder if I can wedge in a question without her guard going up.

I'm about to ask her why she's so jaded, but she talks first. "That must have been so hard for him." She sighs and leans into me. "He was the happiest he's ever been, and to just leave like that. It's terrible."

"Agreed," I nod against the top of her head. "Speaking of…"

"Why do I get the feeling we're about to have an uncomfortable conversation?"

"Because we are, sort of." She moves until she's sitting in front of me. "You don't have to answer, but what happened that made you rebel against relationships? Who hurt you so badly?"

She pulls one of the throw pillows into her lap and groans. This isn't a conversation she wants to have. "You know how I told you that my cousins and I have always been close?"

"Yeah, but I don't see what that has to do with anything."

"Well, Stella has always lived in Austin, but Audrey and I lived in this super tiny town up by the Oklahoma border. I idolized Audrey and in my eyes she could do no wrong. I wanted to be just like her… Until I didn't."

"Okay," I draw out.

"She had a boyfriend, and he seemed like the perfect guy. He always let me tag along with them because he knew I was part of the package with Audrey. Where she went, I went. Well, right before the second semester of their senior year started he dumped her and it *destroyed* her. She wouldn't get out of bed and I had to force her to eat. It was bad."

Tiffany takes a deep breath and continues her story. "The two of them were so involved with each other. They literally did everything together, and there wasn't any room for them to breathe. I was fourteen at the time and all I saw was the pain my cousin went through."

"That had to have been confusing at such a young age. To see someone you love hurting so much."

"It was. But it also showed me not to give all of myself to someone. I knew that if I ever did that, I would open myself up to the heartbreak Audrey went through." She pulls the pillow close to her chest. "That is why I've never gotten into a serious relationship. There's less pain that way. As long as the other person knows that things won't go further than a fun time, then we're good."

Damn. Something she saw when she was a teenager has shaped her whole view of relationships. "Did the guy give her a reason for breaking up with her?"

"Nope. And that was the hardest part for her. A few weeks later she saw him at a party with another girl, and it sent her into a spiral once again."

"So where does that leave us?" I don't want to ask, but I feel like I need to after hearing her story. After finding out just how against relationships she is. "Are we just having a good time, or can you see something more with me?"

She shrugs her shoulders and looks everywhere but at me. "I don't know. I like being with you. You're fun and get me on a level even my cousins and most people in my life don't. All I can say is I'm willing to see where things go with us. I can't make any promises, though."

I guess that's better than hearing her say I'm disposable. "That's good enough for me. At least for right now. We can see what the future holds for us one day at a time." I'm not lying when I say it even though it pains me to utter those words. I pull her back to me and press play on the show. I'll just make damn sure she has no reason to get rid of me.

SEVENTEEN

Tiffany

THE PAST FEW weeks with Spencer have been amazing.
Even though I told him I can't make any promises, he's
choosing to stick around. All while I'm still trying to wrap
my head around why. There's nothing that stands out. I'm
a party girl and have been since I moved out of my
parent's house. Though recently, I've been going out less
and less because I haven't really felt the urge to. I'm
enjoying the dinners and TV marathons with Spencer. We
may have done this thing backwards, but it might have
been what I needed to make me see there's more to relationships. When Justin broke up with Audrey, it made me
lose any hope I had of finding someone for me.

"Tiffany," Dennis calls my name making me jump.

My hand hits my water bottle, knocking it down as
water spills all over the table. "Shit," I mutter, rushing for
the paper towels to clean it up before someone comes in
here and falls.

"I didn't mean to scare you."

I roll my eyes, "Sure you didn't."

"It wasn't my intention, I promise." He grabs the roll of

paper towels and tears off a few sheets to help me. "Your break is over."

"Sorry," I wince. I've never been so lost in thought at work that time flew by so quickly. "I didn't realize it was up. I'll finish getting this cleaned up and head back out there."

"Is everything okay?"

"Yeah," grabbing the towels out of Dennis's hand, I wad them up with my own and throw them in the trash. "Just trying to figure out what makes me girlfriend material."

He places a hand on my shoulder and waits until I look up at him. "I'm sure there are a ton of reasons besides the fact that you are intelligent and kind."

"You're just saying that because you're my boss."

"No, I'm saying it because you're the most dependable employee I have and you've grown leaps and bounds since I hired you." He removes his hand and nods toward the door. "Don't second guess yourself. Y'all are a cute couple."

"Thanks." It's time for me to get out there and do my job. I'll ponder my misgivings later when I'm not at work, which is easier said than done. Why do I keep trying to find ways to sabotage this relationship? It has barely lifted off the ground.

It doesn't help that I got a text from Spencer asking if I wanted to have dinner with his parents. Are we even at that stage yet? This is new territory, and I'm unsure how to navigate it. There's only one person I know actually in a relationship and I need her advice now more than ever.

～

COME ON. *Pick up the phone.* The Dreamcatcher is empty, and it's the only time I can call Stella without worrying about Spencer overhearing me. Or letting him know just how much I'm letting my mind mess with me.

"Wow, long time no talk." She finally answers the phone. "I was wondering if you forgot about me."

"No, I didn't forget about you," I wipe down the table in front of me before putting the chairs upside down on top of it. "I've just been preoccupied."

"I take it things are going well with Spencer?"

"Yeah," I hesitate, wondering if I should even tell her we've started dating. But, I did call her to ask for advice, so I might as well get it all out there. "We're actually dating."

She laughs, and I realize how much I've missed her. I've been so wrapped up in hanging out with Spencer that I haven't made the time to call her like I used to. I can't even remember that last time Audrey and I did Sunday brunch. "I was wondering how long it would be before y'all hooked up."

"It's kind of hard to resist a guy when you've already seen him naked."

"That's very true." I can hear the knowing smile in her voice and I'm happy that she's found her person. "I mean, Johnny was half naked when he came to rescue me from that stupid snake."

I could let her keep talking and put off what I want to talk to her about, but I'm not one to hold my thoughts in. I never have been. "How long were you and Johnny dating before you met his parents?"

She's silent, and I worry she's not going to answer me. "A couple of months, I think. Why?"

"Spencer asked if I wanted to have dinner with his, and I don't know how to respond."

"How long have the two of you been officially dating?"

Ugh, I have no idea. He's been living with me almost three months. "A little over a month?"

"Before I get into that," I can imagine her ticking off the finger with her palm up. "First of all, you better never wait that long to call me again. It's like you get a boyfriend and forget all about me." She takes a deep breath. "Second, if you think it's too soon, then don't agree to it. There's no right, or wrong way to be in a relationship. You just do what your gut says."

"My gut feelings have a tendency to get me in trouble," I argue. "That's the whole reason y'all had to find me a roommate."

"I know. But you're a smart cookie, you'll make the right choice no matter what it is."

"And…" I trail off, not wanting to admit my insecurities. "I'm not even sure what he sees in me. I'm not good girlfriend material. I'm barely friend material."

"Nope," she interrupts me. "Do *not* go down that train of thought. You are amazing. At least, once you get past the temper tantrums and *it's all about me* attitude."

"I'm not that bad." I move on to the next table and clear it off. I don't normally like being here by myself, but tonight I relish it. Spencer and I have been spending so much time together, and work is the only place I've been able to be alone. He hasn't pushed me about committing to more than right now, but I know he wants to.

"Do I need to remind you of the fit you threw when I told you I was *temporarily* moving?"

"In my defense, you did eventually move there permanently. So, you can't throw that in my face." Lifting these chairs is a pain to do with one hand, but I'm not ready to get off the phone with Stella.

"I'll give you that," she sighs. "Just take it day by day. And maybe don't tell Audrey about y'all dating. There's no telling how she'll react since she was so against him living there when she found out you slept with him."

Hiding things from Audrey doesn't sit well with me, but Stella has a point. She's sure to give me a lecture. Telling me how reckless I'm being and that I should end it now. "Okay. I won't tell her. I think if I really want to give this whole relationship thing a shot, I need to do things most couples do. Even if it means an uncomfortable dinner with his parents."

"Why does it have to be uncomfortable?"

"Because what if they know he was meant to be a one-night stand?"

"Oh Tiffany," she laughs. "I'm almost a hundred percent sure he didn't tell them that. If he did, run as fast as you can. That's a definite over share of information to his parents."

"Good point," I concede. "I'll call you and tell you how the dinner goes. I need to finish getting the restaurant cleaned up so I can go home."

There's a knock at the front door, and Spencer is standing outside with a light jacket on. "Okay, Tiff. You better call me more often. I miss you and love you."

"Love you, too." I hang up and go to the door to let Spencer in. "Hey, you." Did I really just say that? If there's anything that will give away he was the topic of conversation, it's that oddly high-pitched statement.

He doesn't comment on it, though. He comes in and

sweeps me in his arms. "I wasn't sure what time you'd be done, so I came early."

I laugh and pull away from him. "You know you don't have to pick me up, right? I've been getting home on my own for some time now."

He rolls his eyes and grins. "I'm perfectly aware of that. But when you work late, I'm not a huge fan of you taking public transportation. So many things could go wrong."

I finish wiping down the tables, and he puts the chairs on top. "Now you sound like Audrey." Sweeping and mopping are the last things on the to-do list and I can go home. The only time my brain doesn't worry over being with Spencer is when I'm actually with him. "I just have a couple of things to finish up and we can leave."

"Anything I can help with?"

"Not unless you've figured out a way to sweep and mop at the same time."

He taps his finger against his chin. "Maybe I'll come up with a program that does just that."

"You'd be a millionaire," I giggle. "Now move out of the way so I can get this done."

Thirty minutes later and I'm locking up the door. It's almost ten-thirty, but people are still driving around the city. I used to be one of those people. Before Spencer, I would head straight to a club, or concert, as soon as I left work. Now, though… I just want to go home and spend time with him. Flashes of Justin and Audrey constantly being together enter my mind, but I do my best to shake them away. This is different. I know my boundaries. At least, I think I do.

Spencer grabs my hand and we walk to his car. "So,

did you give any more thought to eating dinner with my parents?"

"Yes," I answer, slowly. "I'm game. I've never actually done the whole meet the parents' thing so I'm a little nervous."

"You shouldn't be," he gives my hand a reassuring squeeze. "They will love you."

I sure as hell hope so. If they don't, I'm not sure what I'll do. He seems to be close to them, and I don't want to cause a rift. Rather than focus on that on the way home, I think about how nice it will be snuggled up against Spencer, throwing all my self-doubt out of the window. He's been in my bed more often than his own these days, and I'm oddly enough, perfectly okay with it.

EIGHTEEN

Spencer

THE DRIVE to my parents is silent. Tiffany keeps her gaze focused on the window and her knee bouncing nonstop. It's weird seeing someone nervous to meet my parents. They are the most non-threatening people I know. Any past girlfriends I've brought over were eager to meet them. She looks like she wants to hurl herself out of the car while I'm still driving.

I turn the music down and rest a hand on her knee. She stops moving it and looks over at me. "It's going to be okay. You know that, right?"

"No," she shakes her head. "I don't. I'm not sure I can do this." Placing a hand on top of mine, she grips it so hard I'm not sure I'll have blood coursing through it by the time we get there. "I thought I could, but I've never done this before."

"Do you want to go back home?" She doesn't answer me, and I continue, "I can make up a reason we have to cancel. I'm not going to force you to do something you're not ready to do."

Her grip on my hand loosens, and her shoulders relax.

"No, I don't want to go back home. This is normal, I think. Meeting your parents shouldn't be this terrifying."

"You have nothing to worry about." I hope she can hear the sincerity in my voice. "My mom might try to pepper you with questions, but Dad and I will do our best to keep that from happening."

"That doesn't make me feel any better." She groans and drops her head into her free hand.

"You've got this, Tiffany." I give her knee a gentle squeeze. "We'll come up with a code word, and if you feel uncomfortable work it into the conversation and we'll say our goodbyes."

She turns her head, hair hanging in her face, and stares at me. "What did I do to find such an amazing person? I'm not even sure what you see in me."

"I see everything in you." I take the exit to my parents' house, pull into a gas station and put the car in park. "You represent everything I'm too scared to do unless I'm dressed up like my favorite character. You're energetic and live life day to day, never apologizing for enjoying whatever you take on." I sweep the hair out of her eyes, my thumb brushing against her jawline.

"Too bad most of the decisions I make end up making my life, and sometimes other's lives, difficult." She leans into my hand and let's me soothe away her fear.

"Nobody is perfect," I slide my hand under her chin and lift her face until her eyes meet mine. "Well, except for maybe me."

"You are so full of shit," she rolls her eyes and tries to swat my hand away.

Instead of arguing with her, I lean in until my mouth touches hers. She opens up for me, wrapping her arms around my neck, pulling me closer. Well, as close as possible considering the console between us. This feels right. Regardless of whatever fears she has about us or what happened to Audrey, there was a reason I ran into her at that concert then answered that roommate ad.

My phone dings bringing us back to reality. "That's probably my mom wondering where we are."

"I guess," she sighs. "But you can't just kiss me stupid anytime you want to win an argument."

"Is that another rule?"

"Yes," she nods. "Yes, it is. Rule number five, or is it six? Hell, I don't remember anymore. No more kissing if it's to keep me from arguing."

"That goes for you, too."

"Why do you always turn my own rules against me?" She mutters under her breath, but I still hear it. I put the car in drive and continue to my childhood home.

TIFFANY STANDS FROZEN between the passenger door and car. "You know you have to move to shut it, right?"

She nods and stares at my parents' house. "I know that. I'm trying to psych myself up. It's the only way I'll be able to get through dinner." Shaking my head, I grab her hand and pull her away from the car. "What code word do you want to use?"

"Huh," her eyes widen. "What are you talking about?"

"We discussed having a word to bail. Just tell me which word you want to use, and when you say it, we'll go."

"Oh yeah," she taps her finger against her chin. "Let's go with banana."

"Banana?" That's a strange word. How in the hell is

she going to work that into a sentence without it sounding off?

"Yep," she nods her head, and bumps the door with her hip. It slams shut and she jumps. "Sorry, still nervous."

"Don't be." Neighborhood kids are playing in the street. It's a form of hockey and I think about all the times I wanted to join in when I was a kid, but was never invited. Nobody likes the person they assume is a know-it-all because they make good grades. They'd rather exclude that person. I shake the thoughts from my head and bring Tiffany to my side. "They will love you."

She grips my hand so hard my knuckles turn white and takes unsteady steps up the porch stairs. A shadow crosses in front of the living room window, and I know Mom has been watching, waiting for us to decide when we're going to come in. At least she gave us that small bit of privacy. Normally, she'd come out and ask what's taking so long. I send a silent thank you into the air and knock on the door.

"Spencer," Mom says before she completely opens it. "You know good and well that you don't have to knock."

I shrug my shoulders and lean in for a hug. "It's the polite thing to do when I bring a guest."

"You must be Tiffany," Mom reaches around me and grabs Tiffany's free hand. "I've heard so much about you."

"Uh, hi Mrs. Warren," she shakes her hand but Mom hasn't let go and she's becoming uncomfortable. "Spencer has been feeding me all the food you've sent home with him."

"Oh," Mom's eyebrows raise. "I didn't realize both of you were eating them. How did you like them?"

"They were delicious," Tiffany smiles and pries her

hand out my mom's grip. "It's been a while since I've had a home-cooked meal."

"That's a shame." She glances at the kids playing in the street and shakes her head. "What a terrible hostess I'm being. Come on in. I'm putting the finishing touches on dinner, but you can hang out in the living room with Dad. He's watching some show about ancient civilizations on *History Channel*."

We step inside, and I close the door behind us, prepared to lead Tiffany into the living room and hoping mom didn't pull out the baby albums. But Tiffany stops. "Do you need any help?" Considering how terrified she was to come inside, I'm surprised she offered. I glance between her and my mom, waiting for the answer.

"That's so kind of you," Mom finally says. "But, you're a guest. Take some time to relax. There isn't much left to do."

Tiffany's entire body sags in relief. Once Mom is heading back toward the kitchen and I whisper in her ear. "Why did you offer to help?"

"I wanted to give a good impression," she mutters back. "I told you, I have no idea what I'm doing. Offering to help always works in the movies, and I thought it might win me some brownie points."

Bumping into her shoulder, I smile. "She already likes you. You don't have to do anything you're not comfortable with." She sidles closer to me and I wrap an arm around her waist as I lead her into the living room. "Now, it's time to meet my dad."

He's sitting in his favorite recliner, despite how much Mom hates it, she doesn't get rid of it. The chair is leaned back, and an excited voice is talking about ruins at such a loud volume, I cringe. "Dad." He doesn't hear me, and I lean closer. The old man is asleep and I can't stop the laugh from leaving my mouth.

"What's so funny?" Tiffany asks from behind me.

I lean back, and point toward my father's prone figure lying in the chair. "Apparently waiting for us tired him out." I run my hand through my hair. "Or, Mom put him to work this morning, and he's exhausted. One of my favorite things about not living here anymore. No chores."

"And here I thought, I was your favorite part of moving out." She pulls her hand out of mine and crosses her arms over her chest, bottom lip sticking out. Pouting will get her nowhere. "I didn't even know it was you I might be moving in with." I roll my eyes and bend down to my dad again. "Dad," I whisper. "Dad," a little louder this time. I swear this man could sleep through a tornado. This time I grab hold of his arm and shake. "Dad, wake up."

"I'm up, I'm up." He jumps up and almost hits me in the face with his flailing arms. "What did I miss?" He's looking around the room and his eyes widen when he registers that I'm standing in front him. "When did you get here?"

"About five minutes ago," I laugh. "How long have you been asleep?"

Dad runs his hand over his balding head and grunts. "I was only resting my eyes."

"Sure you were." I gesture for Tiffany to step up. "Dad, this is Tiffany," I wave my hand toward her. "Tiffany, this is my dad."

"It's nice to meet you, Mr. Warren." She holds out her hand waiting for him to shake it.

He doesn't, though. He lifts the lever on his recliner until it's back into a sitting position and stands up. "We hug around here." He pulls her into a warm embrace and her eyes go wide. It would comical if I didn't see panic written all over her face. "It's good to meet you, Tiffany."

She untangles herself from his arms and takes two steps back, peeking over at the TV. "What are you watching?"

"Before my eyes closed," he gives me a pointed look. "It was a show on the Mayan ruins. Interesting stuff." Yeah, so *interesting* he passed smooth out while he was watching.

She doesn't say anything right away, instead waiting for the commercial to come to an end. Once the show's title comes up, she leans closer to my dad and whispers, "It looks like the same show is still on. I don't think you were asleep for very long."

That small reassurance means a lot to my dad, and he beams. "We'll keep my small nap a secret. Just between us or his mom will have my butt."

I snort, "I thought you were just resting your eyes."

"Exactly," he winks at Tiffany before telling us to make ourselves at home. I think he forgets that I'm not the guest, but I'm also not going to correct him. Some of the tension Tiffany held while meeting my mom has diminished, and I know she's going to get along great with Dad. Mom can be a little difficult sometimes, especially when things don't go the way she expects them to.

Dad sits back in his recliner and we sit on the couch, our attention on the TV. Tiffany is completely relaxed now that the attention is off of her. She can be in the zone without a single worry. The TV has her full attention, and I didn't realize she liked documentaries. Nothing on her *Netflix* account has suggested that she would. I'm not going to question it, though. It will ruin the moment.

Instead, I place my arm behind her head on the back of the couch, basking in this moment where she's not freaking out and wondering if she's good enough to be a part of my life.

Mom calls from the kitchen, "Dinner's ready." She may try to act like she's little miss hostess, but she's not really. Someone hung up on that title would have walked in here and told us. Not Mom, though. She yells it through the house and expects us to congregate at the dining room table. Dad stands and looks from us to the kitchen. "We better get in there or she'll physically push us to the table."

"We'll be right there," I nod toward my dad. "Can you give us a second?"

"Absolutely," he grins. "I'll help your mother set the table and whatever else she asks me to do."

"Thanks." When he's gone, I turn toward Tiffany. Our knees a mere inch from touching. "Are you ready for this?"

She gulps, and I can see her throat working, wishing it was working for another reason than nerves. "Not really."

"We've got this," I glance toward the hallway that leads to the kitchen. "Remember, our code word is banana. You only need to say it once and I'll sweep you out of here like the damsel in distress you are."

"Pfft." She smacks my arm. "I'm not in distress… yet." Mom's voice is coming from the dining room, and I know we have seconds until she comes looking for us.

"Let's get in there," I reach for her hand to pull her off the couch at the same time I stand up. "The plus side is you get a free home-cooked meal out of this whole ordeal."

As soon as she's standing, Tiffany pulls her hand out of

mine, and straightens her shoulders. "The worst that could happen is your mother hates me, and I'll never be able to look her in the eye again."

She follows me into the kitchen and takes a seat on the side of the table. Mom is at one end and Dad is on the other. I can sit across from Tiffany or beside her. Mom already set my plate on the other side of the table, but I feel like I sit over there I will betray Tiffany's trust in me. However, if I move the plate, Mom might make some snide comments when I come over some other time. Not that I blame her, it's the same seat I've sat in since I was a kid.

In the end I take the seat across from Tiffany. I want to read her facial expressions during dinner. She may not realize it, but her face speaks louder than her words ever could. She raises her eyebrows at me in question, but I grin at her, hoping she knows all is well. This is the best position to read the situation.

Mom passes each dish around, making sure Tiffany gets the first helping. It's her way of making Tiffany feel welcome, but I can see my girl struggling with how much is appropriate to spoon on her plate. She has a pretty healthy appetite, at least from what I've seen. There are times she's eaten more than me.

"What do you do for a living?" Mom asks as she digs into the mashed potatoes on her plate.

"I'm a waitress at The Dreamcatcher, downtown." Her mouth is in a wide smile and I know how much joy that job brings her.

"I see," Mom says, and Tiffany's smile drops. "What do you see yourself doing in the future?" Tiffany's eyes widen, and I can tell she's about to freak out. She wasn't prepared to deal with my mom's nosiness. She doesn't mean anything by it, I don't think. I open my mouth to answer for her, but Tiffany speaks first. "I'm not sure," she shrugs her shoulders. "I haven't thought that far ahead."

"Don't you think—" Mom begins, but Dad cuts her off.

"Honey, they aren't here so you can interrogate the woman who's captured our son's attention. They are here for dinner and so you can get to know Tiffany better."

"That's what I'm trying to do."

Dad only shakes his head and does his best to steer the conversation in a different direction. Focusing all of his attention on me. I glance over at Tiffany, and she's sitting rigid. She smiles when appropriate and nods her head at the right times. She hasn't said the code word yet, but I'm tempted to pull the plug and whisk her away to safety. Somewhere my mom can't reach her. I've never held any resentment toward Mom, but tonight is a new low for her. She's always been pushy and intrusive, except it was always only directed at me. However, I grew up knowing how to handle her when she was in those moods. Tiffany shouldn't have to deal with this crap.

When I make a move to stand, Tiffany subtly shakes her head. She doesn't want to let my mom get to her, but I know she is.

The rest of dinner is relatively quiet. Small talk about the weather and what sports teams we're rooting for this year. It's awkward between these walls, and something I haven't felt before. Not here, anyway.

Tiffany helps me gather the dishes while Mom puts the leftovers into containers for us to take home. She doesn't say anything while we load the dishwasher, just dutifully puts the dishes into the dishwasher, fitting everything in like a puzzle.

Once we're back at the table, Mom puts the pies she

made on the table. As much as I would love some of her homemade pie I can't let Tiffany endure the energy my mom is throwing out there. "We should probably get going." I pat Mom's shoulder and lean in for a hug.

"It's still early, and I'd love to get to know Tiffany better." Mom argues.

"She needs to make some *banana* bread for one of her cousins."

"Well, drat." Mom looks toward Tiffany. "Maybe next time."

We say our goodbyes and are at the door, a bag full of food in my hands. "It was nice to meet you Mr. and Mrs. Warren."

"You too," Mom beams. Dad leans over and whispers something in her ear, a small grin takes over and she nods in agreement.

"Thank you for dinner and welcoming me into your home."

"Come back anytime." What's with Mom's change in attitude? She was grilling her moments ago, but all that has dissipated into nothing. I'll have to call her later and ask her what her deal was.

"I will," Tiffany replies and walks toward the car. Her steps are fast and she almost drops her bag of leftovers as she walks down the stairs. This will be a long drive home.

NINETEEN

Tiffany

THE DRIVE HOME IS SILENT, and I feel horrible. The whole thing was exhausting. I know I put on a tough bravado when I was interacting with Spencer's parents. Inside though… I was a bundle of nerves. Forcing each word out without sticking my foot in my mouth and doing it all with a smile on my face. I don't like how his mom was questioning my work choice. I may not have my whole life planned out but at least I'm happy. For the most part, anyway.

Spencer pulls into the parking garage, puts the car in park and comes around to my side to open the door. I want nothing more than to fall into my bed. He waits until I'm out of the car before grabbing my hand, giving it a gentle squeeze. It is terrifying how well he can read me. My cousins would be finding ways to correct me or give advice, but he gives me silent strength.

As soon as we're in the apartment, he pulls me into his arms. "I'm sorry about my mom," he whispers into my hair. "She's a little overprotective of me."

"It's fine," I say into his shirt. "It went better than I

expected. I just wasn't ready for her to question my choices."

"Is there anything I can do?" He leans back until his eyes meet mine. At least he's not mad at me. He shouldn't be since I didn't respond to his mom, but I can't help but feel like a disappointment.

Most people my age already have their shit together, and I'm only now figuring out how to adult without my parents' help. "I just want to go to bed. I have an early shift tomorrow."

"I'll go get the bed ready," he starts down the hallway but my voice stops him.

"I kind of want to sleep alone tonight."

His face falls, and he tries to recover with a small grin. "Okay. I'll, uh, just get it ready for you, then."

"You don't have to do that." I feel like the worlds biggest bitch for wanting sleep on my own, but I need the space. I rely on him way too much to pick me up when I'm having a bad day. It's not healthy for either of us.

"I want to," he says and continues down the hallway toward my room.

I set my bag on the counter and take stock of what my life has become. It's not bad at all, but I can't help feeling like maybe I rushed into things with Spencer. He's amazing and everything a woman could want. And… I know I'll screw it up.

Spencer hasn't come out of my room yet, and I'm wondering what exactly he's doing. My steps are slow as I make my way down the hallway. When I get to my door, Spencer is stacking the last of the pretty pillows from my bed in a neat pile on my dresser. The comforter is pulled back and my jammies, which consists of a t-shirt and shorts, are on my bed. "Thank you," I whisper.

"Get changed, and I'll bring you some water." How is this man still so incredibly sweet while I know he must be disappointed? If the roles were reversed, I'm sure I'd be pestering him about something and demanding to know why he wants to sleep alone. Further proof I'm not on the same maturity level as him.

I change into my jammies and climb into bed. It's still early, but I just can't bring myself to care about that. Spencer comes back with my water and sets it on the nightstand before pulling the blanket on top of me, tucking me in the way my mom did when I was a kid. "Get some rest."

With that, he walks out of the room, closing the door gently behind him. I pull the pillow he sleeps on toward me and I squeeze it to my chest. It smells like him, and I can't help thinking I've made a huge mistake in asking him to sleep in his own bed. But I ignore that feeling, and snuggle closer to the pillow, hoping for sleep to find me soon.

SPENCER DOESN'T WAKE up before I leave for work. It's that moment I realize I've truly hurt him. I should have sucked it up and let him sleep in the same bed as me, but I needed time alone. Meeting his parents was *not* one of my most favorite things, even if his dad is cool. He stepped in to stop Spencer's mom from badgering me. He'll never know how grateful I am for that kindness.

I open the door to The Dreamcatcher and the smell of fried breakfast meets my nose. This must be what Heaven smells like. "You're cooking early, Dennis," I call out as I pass the kitchen for the break room.

When I walk out, my boss is setting two plates on a table and motions for me to sit. "That's because I'm making my most valuable employee some breakfast."

"Does this mean I get a raise?" I take a seat and stare down the greasy food in front of me. I'm not sure how Dennis knew that I might need a pick me up this morning, but he did. This is one reason he's the best boss ever. Not that I've had many bosses for longer than a few weeks, but he's a large part of the reason I love working here. He fills my parent's role since they are so far away.

"Funny," he deadpans. "But… I might have an opportunity coming up for you soon."

I can't tell if that's good or bad, so I don't respond. "Thank you for breakfast. I definitely needed it."

"Is everything okay?" When I don't respond, he continues, "Are you and Spencer good?"

"I think so." It's the only answer I can give him. "I met his parents over dinner and it didn't go all that well." It wasn't horrible either. I was expecting it to be so much worse.

"Did you say something embarrassing?"

"Not exactly, but his mom is…" What would be the best way to describe her? She's not mean by any stretch, and I can tell she loves her son more than anything. "Abrasive." It's still not the right word, but it's the best I can come up with.

"Ah," he laughs. "I take it you didn't hit if off with her."

"I don't think she likes me very much."

He taps his knuckles on the table and stands up. "Don't worry. She'll come around." With that bit of so-called wisdom, he walks off with his plate in his hand.

I didn't realize I was the type of person others would

have to "come around" to, and it makes me feel kind of shitty. There's no time to dwell on it, though. The diner opens in twenty minutes. I need to scarf down this food and get ready to open the doors.

IT'S ALMOST time for my break. I just need to get this credit card back to the table, and I'll be free for fifteen blissful minutes. The plus side to being busy is not having time to overthink things. I haven't had time to worry over every single second I spent at Spencer's childhood home, wondering if I made an ass of myself, or if his mom likes me.

I'm on my way back to the table when I see Audrey walk through the door. The little bell overhead jingling happily. Too bad the sound doesn't match her expression. She has a tight smile, but when her eyes meet mine, it's with laser focus. *Oh shit.* Did Stella tell her about me and Spencer?

A part of me wants to take the next customer that walks through the door so I don't have to find out why my cousin is here. The other part tells me to shut the hell up. My feet hurt and I need this break. Maybe I can sneak out to the alley and take my break there? Audrey is already coming toward me, and I know avoiding her will be impossible.

"Here's your card," I set the small portfolio holding the card and receipt on the table. "Y'all have a great day." I smile, hoping it doesn't look as manic as I feel.

Audrey follows me to the break room, completely ignoring the employees only sign hanging on the wall next to the door. "Where the hell have you been? You haven't called me in weeks," she barely keeps from yelling.

"I've been busy." I shrug my shoulders, pull out a chair and plop into it.

"You've been busy before, but that's never stopped you from coming over, or at least calling me." Geez, she sounds like my mom when I don't call her back right away. "How are things going with Spencer living there? He's not giving you any trouble, right?" She pulls out the chair next to me and sits down more gracefully than I did. "I just want to make sure Stella and I didn't make a horrible decision about him moving in there after your history with him."

I know Stella told me not to say anything to her, and that it's a bad idea to do it. Except… I can't keep secrets from her. It felt gross when Stella suggested it and feels icky even now. "We're kind of, um, dating each other." I look down at my hands resting in my lap. Like a child terrified of getting in trouble for doing something wrong.

"I'm sorry," Audrey crosses her arms. "Did you say you are *dating* him?"

Her waiting silence is brutal. I don't do well when my cousins are mad at me, but I don't think I can handle the disappointment that is no doubt pouring from her.

"Yes," I say, barely above a whisper. She stands so quickly the chair screeches across the floor, and I know it has to be loud enough for the diners to hear. My shoulders tense at the sound, and I prepare myself for the lecture I know is about to come.

Seconds later, she's pacing back and forth across the small room. "Of all the idiotic things you have done, this might be the icing on the cake. What will happen when you decide you're bored with him and want to move on to someone else?" She pauses, and waits for me to look up before adding, "He is on the lease, Tiffany. It's not like you can just force him to move out because you decided things were getting too real."

"We've already talked about that," I argue. "If things get too heavy, then we'll break it off. Being amicable to each other is better than hating each other's guts."

"By the time things get *heavy*, it's too late to go back to friendship. You realize that, right?" When I don't answer she shakes her head. "Of course you don't. You've never been in an actual relationship. Is he why you haven't made time to talk to me, or come over?"

Her relationship comment is a punch in the gut, and as badly as I want to lash out, I don't. "This right here is why I didn't tell you sooner." My hands are now balled in my lap. Fingernails digging into my skin. "You overreact about everything. It's bad enough that I have my own doubts and fears about dating him. I don't need your negativity adding to it." It's like high school all over again.

Audrey's eyes softened, and she takes small, cautious steps toward me. "I'm not trying to make you feel bad, Tiff." She stops directly in front of me and puts her hands on my shoulders. "I just… don't want to see you get hurt. I don't want you to go through the same heartache I did."

I step back, out of her grasp. "Seeing what you went through in high school is the entire reason I've never let myself get close to someone. I didn't want love to break me." She looks like she's about to interrupt, but I continue full steam ahead. "I'm not saying that I love Spencer because it is way too damn early for that, but I like him… A lot. I can see where you're coming from, and believe me, that thought is stuck on repeat in the back of my head. For now, though, I want to see where this might lead."

Tears filled her eyes, but she doesn't let them fall. "Just, be careful. Don't let yourself become too attached too early. It might come back to bite you in the butt."

With that wisdom, she's gone. All the fight left her when I brought up the way Justin dumped her. Now, I not only have my own fears when it comes to being with Spencer, but also the knowledge that I've hurt my cousin's feelings. Today is shaping up to be fan-fucking-tastic.

Spencer

FINALLY. I'm finished working with the client from Hell. I'm almost certain that man has given me gray hair with all the changes he requested. The app is exactly how he wants it. For now, anyway. I hope I don't hear from him in six months wanting to change the design, again. I can now safely tuck these files away on my external hard drive and move on to another project. There's nothing due for a few weeks, and I'm still waiting to hear back from Dale. I'll lowball my fee if I have to, or figure out some even exchange. Working with Crooked Halo would not only stretch my creativity, but I really want to work with them. Maybe I should I have contacted Dale when Tiffany told me to, but I decided to wait a couple of days. Not wanting to seem too eager.

I glance at the clock. It's almost six, and Tiffany will be home soon. Dinner at a nice restaurant seems like a perfect reward for finishing Mr. Harrison's project, and I know she'll be happy to no longer hear me bitch about him. I'm also hoping a nice night out will go toward mending whatever has broken between us. Things haven't been the same since we had dinner with my parents and I worry they've scared her off. I shouldn't have pushed her to meet them before she was ready. I don't sleep in her room as much as I was, and when I bring my parents up, she tenses up and changes the subject.

The door to our apartment opens and closes, and I run out of my room to greet her. Damn, I'm like an excited puppy, happy their person is finally home. And that's what she is… *My person*. Now, if only I could get her to see that. To show her she's it for me without scaring her off.

She looks exhausted. Her hair is a mess with flyaways coming out of her ponytail. Her usual chipper attitude is nowhere in sight. I grab her bag off her shoulder and set it on the kitchen counter. I'm almost afraid to ask, but I do anyway. "How was your day?"

"Long," she sighs. "Dennis is training me for a new position."

"Oh, yeah?" She didn't mention anything about it before, and the realization sucks. "What is he training you for?"

Tiffany scrunches up her nose. "He hasn't really told me. He just keeps showing me things that he normally does." She shakes her head, "Well, except for the cooking. We all know I'm a lost cause when it comes to trying to feed people."

"It sounds like he wants you to take on a management type of position."

"That's my guess, too." She drags her feet to the living room and falls, ungracefully, onto the couch. "I don't want that kind of responsibility. It's too much, and I don't know if I can handle it."

I sit on the floor next to the couch and take off her shoes. "You can."

"How do you know that?" She doesn't look at me when she asks. Her eyes are fixed on the ceiling.

"Because," I scoot closer to where her head is, and wait for her to turn toward me. Anything to show she does still care. "I see how much work and effort you put into The Dreamcatcher. You know the inner workings more than anyone else aside from Dennis." She finally turns her head toward me, and her gaze meets mine. "He sees that in you, too."

"You have a point," she nods. "I know damn well that Janie wouldn't be able to handle half the things I do. She definitely doesn't care about the job like me." Leaning forward, her lips touch my forehead. A peck before leaning back on the couch. "Thank you for the reminder. I needed it today."

"That's kind of what I'm here for as your boyfriend," I poke her arm. "To pick you up when you're down and make you feel better."

"You're doing a damn fine job of it," she smiles. "How was your day?"

I lean back against the coffee table, and it scoots out from behind me. I fall backward, but throw my arms out to catch myself. She really needs something sturdier in here. Maybe I'll buy her a new one when Dennis tells her she's being promoted. "It's been pretty good, actually." I reposition my arms to even out the weight of my body. "Do you remember that pain in the ass client I'm working with?"

"How could I forget?" I feel her eye roll more than I see it. She's back to staring at the ceiling, and I swear her eyelids are closing then fluttering back open. "You only complain about him every other day. Sometimes multiple times if he's bugging you nonstop."

"There's no need to be a smart ass," I groan.

"You wouldn't have me any other way." The corner of her mouth lifts, but the words are slow and lazy. She's right, though I wouldn't. She challenges me more than anyone else I know, and I always look forward to our random conversations.

"True," I laugh. "Anyway, his project is officially done."

She sits up, holding herself up with her elbows. "That's amazing," she yells. "Now you don't have to worry about his five million fickle decisions. I swear, he changes his mind more than Stella buys shoes."

"I take it she buys a lot of them?"

"Yep," Tiffany pops the *p*. "Though, I don't know what use she's getting out of all those heels since she lives in the country now." She pauses waiting for me to say something. "So, are we going to celebrate or something? I'm sure you've had bigger clients you've worked with, but this one in particular feels like a real victory."

"I was actually going to ask you if you wanted to have a nice dinner when you got home." I lean forward and run my fingertips through the red strands of hair in her ponytail. "But you look like you want to fall into your bed. We can go some other time."

"No way," she plasters on a smile. I can't tell if this one is real or fake, and it's bugging me. "This is a huge deal. No more phone calls from the indecisive guy, and it gives you time to reach out to Crooked Halo. We're going out tonight."

"I've actually already emailed Dale. I'm just waiting to hear from him." I lay my head down on the couch next to her arm. "And we really don't have to go tonight. Only if you want to."

"Let me take a quick shower and get the smell of diner food off of me." She hops up from the couch, suddenly full of energy. "I'll be ready before you know it." Without a backward glance, she races down the hallway.

TIFFANY WANTED STEAK FOR DINNER, so we sit at a steakhouse not too far from the apartment. This wasn't exactly what I was thinking when I said a nice restaurant, but if this is what she wants, I'll do it with a smile. Anything to see her light up again. Things almost feel normal tonight. *Almost* being the keyword. I wish we could go back in time to dinner at my parents' house and I could tell Mom not to look down on Tiffany's job. Especially since she loves it so much. She should never feel ashamed of what she does for a living, and I have a feeling that's what shut her down. It's been almost two weeks, and I'm only now seeing some of her sparkle come back. Why does my mom have to insert herself into every aspect of my life? I'm her son not her friend, even if she wishes I would confide in her more. I'm an adult now, and perfectly capable of making my own choices. Good, bad, or whatever else is in between. Being with Tiffany is *my* choice, and hopefully the two of them can get along one day. It would make things less awkward, but if it doesn't happen, mom will have to get used to it.

"Can you pass the butter?" Tiffany points her knife toward the tiny bowl on my side of the table. The best thing about this place is the bread. It's crispy on the outside, and warm and soft on the inside.

I scoot the butter closer to her, and place my elbows on the edge of the table. We came in late so there isn't much chatter. "When do you think Dennis will officially promote you?"

She shrugs her shoulders. "I don't know." She takes a big bite out of the piece of bread in her hand and moans. The sound kills me. Not sleeping in the same bed as her is my own personal hell. It's not because of the lack of sex, though I miss that too. It's that I enjoy holding her in my arms. Being the one she leans into when she's most vulnerable. Correction. The one she used to lean into before my mom screwed it all up. It's my fault for letting her be so involved in my life. I should have drawn a line in the sand ages ago. I didn't because I was too damn worried I would hurt her feelings. Now she's possibly ruined the best thing that's ever happened to me. "When do you think you'll hear from Crooked Halo?"

I'm so lost in my thoughts that the question takes me by surprise. "I'm not sure."

"How long have you been waiting on a response?"

Crap. I wasn't expecting her to ask this. I wonder how mad she will be when I answer. "A couple of days."

"What?" She shrieks and a couple a few tables down looks in our direction. "They emailed you two weeks ago, and you waited to respond?" She whispers loudly.

"I was scared," I shrug. If anyone will understand my fear of the unknown, it's her. I mean, she didn't date anyone seriously out of fear. I'm not going to voice that, though. It's a sure-fire way to piss her off and watch her stomp right out of this restaurant.

"You have no reason to be scared." She reaches her hand out to place on mine, but thinks better of it and pulls it back. "Your work is amazing, and assuming they haven't found someone else, they'll get back to you soon."

Her actions tonight are confusing. One minute she's

attentive and the next she's reserved. Acting like the Tiffany I moved in with. The back and forth will drive me insane, and I hope this isn't the beginning of the end. I'm too far gone to be friends at this point. I'm falling in love with her, and she doesn't even realize it. At least, I don't think she does. For all I know, our relationship became too much the moment I asked her to meet my parents. I'd ask her what she's feeling, but I don't think she would tell me. She's too busy building up her defenses, once again.

"Let's hope they email me back soon, then." I force a smile and the look on her face is the same as mine. Trying to be happy even though we're both feeling the strain of something we can't identify.

"Give it a few more days." She grabs another piece of bread, slathering it with butter. "They are probably busy writing music or whatever it is bands do when they aren't performing."

The rest of our meal comes and we eat in silence, mostly. The tension isn't something I'm used to with her. Hell, even when we were fighting after I moved in, at least there was emotion behind it. Now there's only a shell of the woman I met that night at the concert. There's no way dinner that night messed her up this much. My bet is someone said something to her, and she's trying to find an easy way out. One that doesn't hurt either of us.

A night that was supposed to be celebratory has turned into something else altogether. I feel nothing but fear. Fear of her shutting down all of her emotions. Fear of losing her before we've even given each other a real shot. Lucky for me, I don't plan on going down without a fight.

TWENTY-ONE

Tiffany

SINCE DINNER THE OTHER NIGHT, Spencer has been relentless about spending time together. It's as if he's made it his mission to fix whatever it is he thinks is broken. I only wish he'd realize that right now. *He* is part of the problem. This is all too much, especially after talking to Audrey the other day. I can't allow myself to be consumed by him. It will only hurt in the end. At the same time, I'm not ready to end things with him. Not ready to say goodbye to the one good thing in my life.

"Order up," One of the cooks Dennis hired calls out. Honestly, I need to stop getting inside my head when I'm at work. It's starting to affect my tips.

I grab the plates and set them on my tray before balancing it on my hand. "Thanks," I say over my shoulder. The food on the tray makes my mouth water. I haven't eaten all day because we've been so busy. I didn't even get to take my full break earlier. Hopefully, the kitchen staff can whip something together for me to take home. I glance at the big clock on the wall on the way to the table. Only an hour left, and I get to leave for the day. The extra shifts are definitely padding my bank account, just in case the inevitable happens and I'm left without a roommate again. I need to prepare for the worst. I don't want to be a mess like Audrey was and calling my parents for money is *not* an option.

A young couple and their toddler son are seated at the table, and I take my time setting the plates down in front of each of them. "And these yummy chicken tenders are for you." The little boy is so excited and clapping his hands as I place the plate in front of him. "Be careful, though. The plate is a little warm." He beams at me and grabs one of the tenders and dips it in the gravy.

"Adam," his mother admonishes. "What do you say?"

He pauses, chicken almost to his mouth, "Thank you, ma'am." Wow, this kid speaks so clearly. Maybe he's a little older than I first thought. Either way, his thanks makes me feel better.

"You're very welcome," I smile at him. "Let me know if y'all need anything else."

"We will, thank you." It's customers like these that make me love my job. Sliding the tray under my arm, I head back toward the food counter.

Janie is there, putting an order in for one of her tables. "Hey, Tiffany. How is everything?"

"Good," I drawl.

"That's good." She turns until she's facing me. "I was just wondering because you've been here a lot again."

"Just trying to save some extra money," I say, voice tight. Not that it's any of her business. "The way things are going with my cousin and her boyfriend, I'm sure I'll be buying wedding attire soon enough." It's not a complete lie. I have a feeling Johnny will pop the question sooner rather than later. Those two are definitely meant for each other.

"Wow. I didn't realize it was that serious for them." She tightens her ponytail. "It's a good reason to save money, though."

"The fact that he drove all the way down here to win her back, and she moved to where he is, I'd say it's always been that serious for them." I take a deep breath. "I guess when you know you've found the one, you'll do anything for that person."

"Is it like that with you and the hottie that came in here?" She's not trying to be malicious or anything. It's an honest question and I don't know how to answer it.

"Not really," I finally say. "We're just having fun and seeing where things go." And this is the biggest lie I'll tell myself all day. I feel more for him and it's terrifying. I'm saved from having to say more when the hostess seats another table in my section. "I better get back to work."

"Alright," she gives me a small wave. "I'll catch up with you later."

Not if I can help it. She's making me think about things I'm not ready to face. And that's how the rest of my shift goes. Staying busy and avoiding Janie.

SPENCER IS on the sofa watching TV when I come through the door, and I can't stop myself from admiring the way he looks so comfortable in my life. That is until the fear bubbles up, and takes over my brain. "Hey," I call out, in case he didn't hear the door open.

He jumps up, and rushes into the entryway, wrapping me in his arms. "How was your day?"

It wasn't horrible, but I don't want to let him know just how much I've been trying to distance myself from him. So, I pull myself away from him and hold up the bag of food in my hand. "I brought dinner."

"Fantastic," he says, grabbing the bag from my hand. "I'll get some plates and silverware. Sit down and relax."

"Thanks." I walk to the living room and notice everything is put away. All the little odds and ends I've left out and haven't put up. The stray clothes I've left in my wake when folding laundry. All of it is gone. "It's really clean in here." I want to feel like I'm contributing, but anyone who *knows* me, knows that I hate cleaning. If I could afford it, I would hire someone to come in and hit the big things that I put off.

"Yeah," his voice is hesitant. "I needed something to do while waiting for a response from Dale. I finished working with another client and got tired of sitting at my computer hitting refresh on my email."

Now for the important question. "Did you touch any of my food in the refrigerator?" Please say no. He knows I don't like anyone messing with my food.

"No," he rushes out. "Everything is still in there." Good. I'm glad he didn't throw anything out. "You don't have much in there except snacks since we've been eating stuff my mom has sent over."

"I'll go through the freezer this weekend. I'm pretty sure some of that ice cream isn't any good."

"Sounds good. I know better than to touch your beloved *Ben & Jerry's*," he laughs.

I toss my bag on the floor beside the coffee table, dirtying up the tidy space. Maybe I'll install some kind of hook by the entryway to put my bag when I get home so it isn't just lying wherever I chuck it. It feels nice to sit down.

My feet are aching and I wonder if I should get some new shoes. It's the one thing about waitressing that I despise. The need to buy new shoes whenever my feet hurt. "You still haven't heard from Dale?"

"No," he sighs. "I sent a follow up email, though. Hoping maybe the first one got lost in cyberspace."

"He'll get back to you," I lean back and close my eyes. I kind of don't want to go into work tomorrow. "He wouldn't have reached out to you in the first place if he didn't want to work with you."

"I hope you're right." His voice is closer and I open my eyes. "Here's your dinner. What do you want to watch?"

"I'm good with anything." I yawn and scoot into the corner of the sofa until I find the perfect level of comfort. "I can't guarantee I'll make it through the whole movie."

"You need to take some days off," he says, sheepishly. Hinting at what I already know I'm doing. Avoiding alone time with him as much as possible. I swear avoidance is my middle name. He picks up the remote and presses play on the movie he was watching. It's one I've seen, so I don't make a big deal about starting something from the beginning. "I hope this is okay."

"It's fine." I dig into my dinner. I really need to stop skipping meals because I'm going through this plate of food way too fast, and I have no doubt I'll feel like crap after I'm done.

The TV is booming with spaceships flying through the galaxy, and I set my plate on the coffee table before getting comfortable in my corner of the sofa again. My legs are tucked under me, with my feet poking out. Normally, I would be curled up next to Spencer, with his arms wrapped around me. Tonight, though, I just can't bring myself to pretend like I'm okay. Like I'm not freaking out with each day that he's pushing to get closer. He seems to sense this and stays on his side of sofa, but he reaches out and places a hand on my foot. "So," he breaks the silence between us. "They've announced the date for Austin City Limits Festival. One of my clients reached out to ask me if I wanted some of the tickets he has for the whole festival. I just need to let him know soon."

That wakes me up. I've wanted to go to ACL for a long time, but my ass has always been too broke to even consider buying tickets. At the same time, the event is months away, and I don't even know if I'll be with Spencer when the time comes. Hell, I don't know if we'll be together for the rest of the month. "Let me check with Dennis and see if I can get off that weekend. We're usually slammed during festival weekends and he wants as many of us there as possible."

His face falls. I hate that I've disappointed him, but he's talking *long-term relationship*. I'm barely cut out for whatever it is we have going on now. "Just let me know as soon as you can so he doesn't offer them to someone else."

"I will." I need to let Audrey's hurt get out of my head. Just because she was destroyed after being so wrapped up in a guy doesn't mean I will. The fear is still there, though. Until working at The Dreamcatcher, I never even held down a steady job because I can't commit to anything. We watch the rest of the movie in silence. It's weird having this chasm between us and not knowing what to do to close it. Before the movie is over my eyes close and I fall into a fitful sleep.

TWENTY-TWO

Spencer

I'M TRYING HARD NOT to let Tiffany's actions hurt me. She's scared, and I get that. Hell, I am too. Never has a woman stuck around this long. She doesn't make fun of my comic collection or the fact that I like cosplay. She seems to *really* get me. If only she could get over the hurt her cousin felt all those years ago. It's crazy to me she's carried this view on relationships her entire life. This fear is so ingrained in her she won't even give us a fair chance.

I am doing my best to think about something else, but it isn't working. Scrolling through color options for my client is doing nothing to quell my frustration. Hell, I'm not even sure what time she'll be home since she's working a double.

Any hope that I was showing her relationships aren't all that bad are dying a slow, miserable death. Nothing I've done has helped. If anything, she's pulling back with each day that passes, and I don't know how to fix it. If I keep pushing, I'll lose her forever. I know that, and I still can't stop trying to spend all my free time with her. This has always been my problem when it comes to women. I put more effort into relationships than they want or are ready for. Then I end up with a broken heart and a lot of time wasted.

My computer dings with an email, and I minimize the window open on my computer. It's also ridiculous that I'm waiting next to my computer for an email like a teenager waiting on a phone call from their crush. All I know is that I want to work with Dale, and Crooked Halo, more than anything right now. I've worked for some high profile companies, and it's this small band that has me anxious.

I open my email and nearly fall out of my chair in excitement seeing Dale's name on the unopened email. *Calm down, Spencer. You don't even know if you have the job yet.* I move my mouse over the email. The small arrow hovering until finally, I click it.

Hey Spencer,

Sorry I haven't answered sooner. We were recording some music. We're definitely on board for you to design our website. Could you also tie everything in with our social media, too? We were approached by someone wanting to sign us, but we need to have a consistent "brand," whatever that is. Can you help us out? We'll be happy to pay your fee and throw in admission to some of our shows.

-Dale

Tiffany was right. They were just busy. I jump out of my desk chair and throw my hand in the air. Victory is mine! Before I reply to Dale, I want to let Tiffany know. I could wait and tell her when she finally makes it home, but it's too exciting not to share now.

Spencer: Guess who's designing a site for Crooked Halo?

I'm not sure when she'll reply. She usually texts me on her breaks, or when she has a free moment. It all depends on how busy they are. So, I'm surprised when my phone dings a minute later.

Tiffany: I told you. Congrats!
Spencer: Want to go out to eat to celebrate?
Tiffany: Actually, a couple of the girls asked if I wanted to grab a drink after work. Raincheck?
Spencer: Sure.

What else am I supposed to say? I didn't even realize she hung out with anyone from work. She hasn't done that in the time we've been together. If it had been Audrey asking her out, I wouldn't think twice about it. But she's never once mentioned going out with any of the girls at The Dreamcatcher. I wonder if Janie is also going because from my understanding Tiffany doesn't get along with her. I could press for more information, but I don't want to freak her out more than I have already. Or, at least I assumed I have. There's no time to stress over it though. I need to email Dale again.

Dale,

Absolutely. I can do anything you need me to do. As far as branding, that's the overall look you want to portray. If you have time, my evening is wide open. We can meet and go over everything y'all want. Just let me know.

-Spencer

His reply comes back.

Sure. Meet at Rob's around 7.

The lack of a greeting bugs me, but I don't want to ask them to change who they are because I like things a certain way. I need to get over it. I have the opportunity to help lift an up-and-coming band to a larger audience. I'd be crazy not to take it up. I wonder if I should let Tiffany know. A part of me wants to leave her wondering where I am in retaliation of the way she's been with me, but I can't do that. It's not who I am.

Spencer: I'm meeting with Crooked Halo tonight. I'm not sure when I'll be home, but it shouldn't be too late. Tiffany: Have fun.

That's it. Two little words, and nothing else. Instead of dwelling on that, I pull up *Photoshop* and start pulling colors and images into a blank document to show the band. It won't be set in stone, just a general idea how things they might like that relates to them.

DALE and the rest of Crooked Halo are sitting in one of the few booths at Rob's bar. I used to wonder why he would give up that precious space that could be used for additional standing room at shows. When I asked him one day, he said it's for those people that love coming to see live shows but don't want to be a part of the crowd.

He basically described me. Hell, the only reason I was in the pit the night I met Tiffany is because my friend needed someone to go with him. We aren't even that close. He just didn't want the ticket to go to waste. He's also the one that bailed on me for Comic Con. Not that I'm mad about any of it. It led me to Tiffany.

There's a band warming up on the stage as I walk toward the booth. The crowd is almost non-existent. I don't know if it's because it's a weeknight, or because nobody wants to take a chance on them. Who knows? I do feel kind of bad for them, but they aren't who I'm here to see.

I pull out the chair at the end of the booth. "Hey guys, thanks for meeting me."

"Anytime," Dale says. "What do you have for us?"

I pull my laptop from the bag I carried with me. Opening it up, I turn it to face them. "This is the color scheme I came up with."

"What is the yellow? I'm not sure how I feel about that."

"It's just an accent color to keep it from looking so dark. And it really ties the blue and gray together." Oh shit. I'm losing them. I thought the yellow would work. Maybe they want to stick to the stereotypical grunge look. I really need to sell them on this color. "I've listened to y'all play, and I've seen you perform. We can take the yellow out and you'll have the same branding look as every other band out there. Or… You can keep it and set yourselves apart. It's your call, but this fits your playing style. You aren't heavy, but you're also not timid. These color choices fit you perfectly."

They sit quietly, looking from my laptop screen then at each other. There isn't a word uttered between them, and the only sound is the band warming up. They all turn toward Dale and nod. "Are you sure you aren't a salesman?"

"Yeah," I look at the band, confused. "Why?"

"Because you've just sold us on using yellow in the branding. What else do you need from us?"

Yes. That's exactly want I wanted to hear. "Do you already have a logo for the band?"

"Not really," Dale answers. "We tried drawing something up a few times, but none of them stuck. We've just been saying who we are since we don't have any merchandise at the moment."

"Is creating a logo for you something you'd like me to do as well?"

"Actually, that would be great," Dale sighs in relief. "It is better if we can keep everything with one person who will make it all cohesive. Thank you so much, man. Shoot me an email with the total, and I've got you."

"I'm excited to be working with y'all." I'm turning into a fanboy and I have no clue why. This isn't some character I love in a movie, or comic character. Being able to do something that broadens my creativity has me all giddy. "If we don't need to talk about anything else, I'm going to head out. Hopefully, my girl is home by the time I get there so I can share the news with her."

Dale grins knowingly. "Is that the redhead that was here with you that night we played?" He shakes his head. "She's one of those music lovers that really gets it. She feels the words as they are being performed. She's the fan all bands want to have. Get home to her."

"Thanks, man," I reach my hand out and shake his. "I'll send you all the details and the mockups as soon as I'm done." It is nice hearing someone else talk about

Tiffany like that. Her passion is why I fall for Tiffany more and more every day. It's those qualities that make her worth fighting for.

~

Damn. She's not here yet. I'm not sure if I should text her or not. I don't want to seem like I'm forcing her to check in with me, but she hasn't gone out since we've been together. Well, other than the night when she was at Audrey's place and then when she went out with that one dude. Luckily, it didn't end well for him since she left their date and ended up in bed with me.

The apartment is quiet without her here. Although, lately, it's been that way even if we are in the same room. Whatever is breaking down between us needs to fix itself. Or she needs to tell me what I'm doing wrong. I've been in relationships before, but they've always been short-lived. Tiffany thinks she is the only one freaking out about us being an item. Being with someone who gets me is new to me. I have just as much reason to be worried about a broken heart as she does.

Spencer: Just wanted to let you know I'm home. Hope you're having fun.

There. That isn't too intrusive. I keep expecting my phone to ding. Any second now. But it doesn't. It's silent in my hand. I can't sit here and watch my phone until she decides she's going to answer me. For all I know she can't hear it over the music. Instead, I'm going to get to work on the logo for Crooked Halo. It should keep my mind off things, at least for a bit.

I turn my computer on, and wait for it to load. Rather than sit in my room and feel suffocated by the tiny room, I'll set up shop in the living room. I'll be able to hear Tiffany come in, and the space is more open. I can spread out across the coffee table and turn the TV on in the background. It resembles the setup I had when I lived in the apartment above the garage. For whatever reason, I think better when I'm like this. The laptop and a notepad are on the coffee table, side by side. My Dr. Pepper is next to it, and I'm sitting on the floor. The computer is still lower than my vision, and I have to look down, but I'm okay with that. I grab the remote and turn on the first thing that pops up under Tiffany's recommendations. It's some rom-com, and I laugh at the suggestion because that is so not the girl I know. She only watches them at Audrey's. I wonder if Audrey forgot to switch profiles when she last watched. Oh well, I'm not actually going to watch it. I have work to do.

Hours have passed and I still haven't heard from Tiffany. I'm getting worried now. It's after midnight and she hasn't answered my text. A part of me wonders if I should text her cousins. They may be able to get ahold of her before I can, but I don't want to be a bother. Hell, I'm not entirely certain they even know we're dating. She hasn't mentioned them much lately. My fingers hover over the keyboard on my phone. It's not absurd if I text her now, right? I mean, it's not like I've been blowing up her phone while she's hanging out with her friends. I don't want to be that guy that makes his girl lose her friendships, but I'm genuinely concerned. What the hell. The most that will happen is Tiffany will be pissed off. I can handle that. It's preferable to any other alternative.

Spencer: Just checking in. I haven't heard from you and wanted to make sure you're good.

I hope she answers me soon. I'm not sure I could go to sleep without at least knowing that she's okay. I save my work on the progress I've made for Dale. There are five different logos I've created for them to choose from. I could send them over to him now, but I'll wait until tomorrow. Right now, all of my concern is focused on Tiffany.

Another hour goes by and there's been no response. I have no other choice than to text one of her cousins. I'm happy I have both phone numbers saved from when I answered the ad for the apartment. Now to decide on which cousin to ask. Audrey acted like she didn't like me much, and I'm better Stella is a safer bet.

Spencer: Hi Stella, I'm not sure if you saved my number, but it's Spencer. Have you heard from Tiffany?

My phone rings in my hand immediately after the text delivers. "Hello," I answer cautiously.

"Spencer," Stella's voice is panicked. "What's happening with Tiff?"

I didn't realize she would call me back. I didn't intend to alarm her, and I'm ninety percent sure I've done just that. "I'm not sure," my voice cracks. "She told me earlier that she was going out with friends from work, but I haven't heard from her since. I figured she would be home by now. She hasn't answered either of the messages I sent her."

Stella groans on the other end of the line. "Damn it," she mutters. I don't think I was supposed to hear that, even though I did. "When is the last time you sent her a message?"

"About an hour ago, I think."

"Fingers crossed she just can't hear her phone. Or, that she's still with her friends." She signs and mumbles something to someone. I'm assuming it's the guy she was with before I moved in. "I wish I could say this is out of the ordinary for her, but it's not. She has a habit of not answering anyone when she goes out. It drives Audrey crazy because her mind always goes to the worst scenario."

"You aren't exactly making me feel better." In fact, she's making me worry more than I was before. I want to go to every bar in the area and search for her. That would most likely freak her out, though.

"Sorry." She pauses for a second. "Let me try to get ahold of her and I'll call you back. If I can't, then Audrey may know what's going on since she lives closer."

"I don't know about that. She hasn't hung out with Audrey much since we've become a couple." Shit. Does she know? "I didn't mean to say that."

"It's okay," Stella laughs. "I already knew. I'm happy she has someone looking out for her, though."

"Thanks." I check the hallway to see if she might have come in while I've been on the phone, but no such luck. "I'll let you know if I hear from her."

"Same. I'll touch base with you later." She doesn't say goodbye, just hangs up. Even though it's a pet peeve of mine, I'm not upset about it. She wants to figure out what's going on as much as I do.

The night grows later, and there's still no word. Stella is doing what she can from Asheville. It's mostly just calling her repeatedly. Even Audrey is trying to get ahold of her to no avail. Her cousins mentioned that she was careless over the night, but I don't want to believe that. I don't want to acknowledge that she didn't have the forethought or need to let me know what's going on. Instead, I'm pacing the apartment waiting for the door to open. Waiting for her to come in with some explanation.

The early morning light is coming in through the windows and my blood is boiling. I've done my best to let her know what's going on with me. If I'm going to be late, I tell her. If something comes up, I give her a heads up. But I've never not communicated with her.

Finally, the door opens. I grab my phone and send a text to Stella.

Spencer: She just walked in.

I'd love to know what kind of excuse she has for me right now.

TWENTY-THREE

Tiffany

SON OF A BITCH. Spencer is awake, and he does *not* look happy.

"Where the hell have you been? I've been worried sick all night thinking something horrible had happened to you."

"I'm sorry," I say just above a whisper. "My phone died, and I passed out when we got back to Janie's place."

"And she didn't have a charger you could use?" He runs his hands through his hair and pushes his glasses up his nose. "Or you couldn't text me from her phone? Something to let me know that you were okay. I've been on and off the phone with your cousins all night trying to figure out where you were."

Hold up. Did I hear him correctly? "You called my cousins?" Anger rushes through me. "You had no right to get them involved."

"What else did you expect me to do?" He throws his hands up in the air. "You weren't answering me, and it was after midnight. I figured if anyone knew what was going on with you, it was them. You told me y'all were close."

"We are, but in case you haven't noticed, I haven't been spending much time with either of them." The reason doesn't need to be said aloud. We both know it's because of him I haven't made time to talk to either of them. I drop my bag in the middle of the floor. I'm tired, feel like crap, and I still smell like the food cooked at The Dreamcatcher. "You shouldn't have called them. I'm a big girl and can take care of myself. I've been doing it for years."

"Yeah? And where has that gotten you?" He motions to himself. "I've done nothing but try to show you how special you are. To break down your walls and hope you realize that not all relationships are doomed to fail. But you don't seem to care. You'd rather go out all night, with a girl you can barely stand, rather than spend any time with me. I never asked you to give up everything you did for fun when we started dating."

I stomp toward him and poke my finger at his chest. "You didn't give me much choice either. You wanted to spend every moment we could together. Not once thinking I might need room to breathe." My voice is becoming loud and shrill. "I used to go out all the time. I did whatever I wanted without feeling like I needed to check in with someone like they were my parent."

Spencer backs away and waves his hands between us. "I can't," he stops for a second and shakes his head. "I can't do this right now. Not until I've calmed down." He walks down the hallway and into his room. Moments later he comes back out with his keys and wallet in his hands. "I'll be back later."

He doesn't say anything else. Just walks out the door, slamming it behind him. I grab my keys out of my pocket and hurl them at the door. Does it solve anything? No. But I don't know what else to do. My emotions are all over the place.

How did this become my life? This exact moment is what I've worked so hard to avoid my entire adult life. I lean against the wall and slide down until my ass hits the ground. The apartment is so quiet now that *he's* not here. I don't know what to do with myself. A tear slides down my cheek and I wipe it away. Another one follows and soon they are flowing with no end in sight. I give up trying to wipe the wetness away.

This is why I don't get involved with men. I never thought I'd get so attached to Spencer. That he'd be the one to ground me in ways my cousins have failed at year after year.

Sitting on the floor crying isn't going to solve anything, though. I got what I wanted. He is most definitely backing off. The crappy part is he may never come back. When I told myself I wanted space, this isn't exactly what I had in mind.

I wipe the tears from my cheeks and stand up. I feel gross. Not to mention the fact that the bottom of my shoes are sticky from the floor at the bar. I need to wash off last night, and now this morning, away. Maybe a shower will make the day a smidge better. I doubt it, though.

Standing up, I grab my bag off the floor and trudge to my room. The first order of business is charging my phone. If he really called Stella and Audrey, I'm sure I have a shit ton of messages from them. And I'm a hundred percent sure none of them are warm and cuddly. There's no way in hell I'm waiting around for the phone to charge so I can read them. A shower is much more important.

Grabbing some towels from the linen closet, I walk to

the bathroom. The bright light is hurting my eyes and I can't remember drinking ever causing me to feel the way I do right now. Achy, tired, and a headache from Hell. It just proves that my tolerance has gone down since I started dating Spencer. All those nights that I used to hit the bars were spent binge watching TV, talking about nothing important, or in my bed. I miss him and the fact that he's not likely coming back hits me like a ton of bricks.

I turn on the bathtub faucet and wait for the water to get warm. Peeling off a layer of clothing with each passing second is like stripping off all the bad decisions I made last night. The first was agreeing to go out with Janie. I've only hung out with her a few times, but she parties more than I ever did. She's the only person I've ever met that can out drink me. If I were responsible, I would have left the bar after two drinks. But, no. I'm the dumbass that ran from their problems and drank way more than I should have. I'm just happy that Janie let me sleep off the hangover on her couch instead of pushing me into an Uber when I couldn't even think straight. Even if it cost me a relationship. One that I'm no longer certain I want out of.

Steam fills the bathroom, and I adjust the temperature. Being scalded on top of everything else would make this day so much worse. I lift the little knob that turns the shower on and step in, pulling the curtain closed behind me. The water pouring down on me feels amazing, and it almost erases everything from my mind, except the way Spencer looked when we were fighting. The resolve on his face when he walked out the front door. And here I go again. It doesn't count as crying if the tears mix in with the water… Right?

∿

My phone is ringing when I turn off the blow dryer. I already know who it is when I pick it up and swipe it open. "Where the hell have you been?" Audrey's voice screeches over the phone.

"Do we have to do this right now? It's already been a shitty morning." I flop onto my bed, waiting for whatever tongue lashing she's about to give me. It's not going to be pretty, and loathe as I am to admit it, I deserve it.

"Yes, Tiffany." Her words are biting and I flinch. "We absolutely have to do this right now. We were up all night worried about you. I tried calling every bar you frequent to see if you were there. With every *no*, I freaked out even more. Wondering if you were in a ditch somewhere, or if someone had taken you."

I'm going to regret putting my two cents in, but I can't help it. "You realize I'm not a child, right? You don't need to parent me on stranger danger."

She keeps going. As if she didn't hear a word I said. "And poor Spencer. I can't imagine how angry he is. After that big show you put on about how important he is, and you stay out all night without letting him know anything."

Audrey is still yelling at me as I press the red circle ending the call. She'll get to flog me in person soon enough. I pull random clothes from drawers and throw them in a pile on the bed. There's no way in hell I'm staying here until I figure shit out. The thought of running into him packing up his stuff is too painful. I never meant for *this* to happen. We had a good thing going, and I let my fears screw with my head. Janie was just an excuse for me to run from my problems yet again.

Searching under my bed for a bag, my hand clamped around something soft and I pull it toward me. It's one of

Spencer's shirts. In all honesty, I should go put it on his bed. I mean, it is his and I'm sure he'll want it back when he inevitably comes to pack up all of his belongings. But… I'm not that strong. I need the shirt as a reminder of the one time I've ever let myself fall for someone. Who cares if I totally screwed it up and let him slip right through my fingers because I'm immature and don't know how to deal with my feelings?

Using my other hand I reach back under my bed and finally find the strap to my duffel bag. I yank it out before standing up and putting my clothes into it. Hopefully, this is enough to get me through at least a couple of days. I can get anything else I might need from Audrey. The zipper is halfway closed when I lay my eyes on Spencer's shirt once again. Lifting it up to my nose, I inhale his scent. It smells woodsy and clean and my heart breaks because I'll never get to smell that again. At least not with him.

With my bag packed, I grab my purse and head toward the living room. A part of me wants to leave him a note and apologize profusely. Telling him he may have been one of the best things that's ever happened to me and that I was falling for him. But I'm not going to. This is what happens in all those romance movies Audrey forces me to watch, and they are not real life. If I am being honest, he's most likely better off without me in his life. He doesn't need someone who can barely take care of themselves.

With one final glance around the apartment, I walk out the front door. Locking it behind me while a tear escapes down my cheek. Hopefully Audrey isn't so pissed off at me she won't let me stay with her. At least for a bit.

~

I KNOCK on Audrey's door and it swings open so hard that the knob hits the wall. I'll be surprised if there isn't a hole in it after that.

"Are you kidding me right now?" She stands in front of me with her arms crossed over her chest, barring my entrance. "You honestly think I'm going to let you come here and stay after you hung up on me in the middle of my rant?"

I shrug my shoulders and nod. "I was kind of hoping that you would overlook that and be happy to yell at me in person." My fingers are crossed that she'll let me in. Give me sanctuary from my own dumbass mistakes.

Audrey's foot is tapping, and normally that isn't a good sign, but finally she gestures for me to come in. "Fine. Don't think I'm through with you, though. I have a lot of words that need to penetrate your thick skull."

I step over the threshold and push my way past her. "Can it wait until I get settled in? The past twenty-four hours have been a complete shit show." Throwing my bag on the floor next to the sofa, I turn toward my cousin. "Please tell me you have something with alcohol."

"Yeah, that's what got you in the mess you're in. I'm not giving you any." She picks up my bag and begins carrying it toward the spare room. "I'll give you a small reprieve, but that's only because Stella should be here soon."

Son of a bitch. This isn't going to be good. Maybe staying here isn't a good idea. Too bad it's my only option.

TWENTY-FOUR

Spencer

SHE DIDN'T EVEN TRY to defend herself. Not that I gave her much of a chance to do that, but it would have been nice if she would have fought me on it at least. Mom has been hovering at the door of the garage apartment. If I'm being honest, some of the problems between me and Tiffany started with her. Not that it's at all her fault Tiffany went out last night and didn't come home. Tiffany is the one who didn't send a simple text message, or call me, to let me know what was going on. Instead, I got to spend my night on the phone with her cousins and worrying something had happened to her. I never believed she was as irresponsible as she claimed until I saw her walk through the door this morning.

"Spencer?" There's a knock on my door and my mom doesn't wait for me to allow her entrance. She barges right in without a care in the world. Not that she needs my permission since I don't technically live here anymore and it is her property. "Are you okay? Is there anything you need?"

That is the million-dollar question. What I need is for

Tiffany to grow up and realize what is right in front of her. I need her to understand that there isn't anything to be afraid of, and even if she is, I'm not going anywhere. Well, I guess I actually did kind of go somewhere. But, I didn't want to say anything that I couldn't take back. "No, just let me wallow in peace." I've never been one to drown in misery with alcohol, but right now I could really use a twelve pack or two.

Apparently my mother does not know the definition of peace, or has the capability to allow me space. She sits down beside me on the old ratty couch and wraps her arm around my shoulders, pulling me close to her like she did when I was a child. Back then it was comforting. Now, it's annoying. "Whatever it is, the two of you can work it out. I know I wasn't the kindest when I was peppering her with questions but I like her. She's unapologetic, and I could tell that she cares about you a lot. I just needed to know that she was right for my baby boy. It's difficult entrusting someone else with your happiness."

"Well," I sigh. "She sure has a funny way of showing it." And it's nice to hear that Mom didn't actually have anything against Tiffany. If only she would have gone about it differently.

"She'll come around. She looks at you the same way I looked at your father when we were young. I know love when I see it."

Groaning, I slide away from my mother. "That's the thing, Mom. I don't think she loves me. She's so terrified of relationships. After we had dinner with you and Dad, she put up wall after wall." I didn't mean to say that last part, but I also want her to know that she's part of the reason Tiffany freaked out.

"That was a couple of months ago. Surely that wasn't

what scared her away now." She taps her fingers against her chin. "Did you do something differently? Or maybe something she didn't like?"

"Not that I know of." I stand up and pace around the tiny room. "Everything was okay. She was a little skittish after dinner since y'all were the first parents she has ever met. But I thought things were going great. Until she started picking up extra shifts again and then last night happened. I don't know what the hell I did."

"Wow," Mom gasps. "You weren't kidding when you said she doesn't do relationships." She shakes her head still astonished about Tiffany's lack of boyfriends, when she smiles. "Why don't you give me her phone number, and I'll call her. Maybe I can get to the bottom of it and figure out what's going on. I hate seeing you like this."

I throw my hands up in the air. "Not. Going. To. Happen." Shaking my head, I continue pacing. "That would overstep your boundaries. Hell, that would be leaping over them and would probably freak her out even more." I take a deep breath and run my fingers through my already disheveled hair. "I'm going to give her some time and let her figure out what it is she wants." In the end I hope it's me.

"I was just trying to help," she huffs. Without another word she stands and leaves the apartment. I swear that woman might be more impossible than Tiffany. Now to figure out how much time to give her. First, I will need clothes in case this is more than temporary.

Our apartment is dark and quiet. The hum of the refrigerator my only soundtrack. She isn't here and my heart sinks. I had all of my hopes pinned on her still being here when I showed up. But that was obviously too much to hope for.

Should I stay and see if she comes home? Or, do I let her have some space? The questions bounce around in my head, and I don't know what to do. I head toward the living room, seconds from sitting down on the couch when I stop. No, I told my mom I would give her room to think, but damn, it's hard. I know what I want. I know *who* I want. I just need her to realize she wants the same thing. Maybe I'm hoping for something that will never happen.

The fact that she isn't here speaks volumes. I search every room for a note or some sign that she's coming back. But, I leave each area of the apartment empty-handed. It's not like she's never going to come back since she is the main signer on this place. The question is when she'll come back. Either way, my heart hurts knowing that she left. She didn't even bother to stay and fight for me…for us. I guess, she got what she wanted. And now I'm left to mend my battered heart.

I go to my room and pack a few days' worth of clothes. There's no way I can stay here. Or, live with her. Not now. Not when she can't be mine. I'm not going to screw her over though. There are still a few months left with me on the lease, and even though her actions are breaking my heart, I will pay my part of the rent, whether or not I live here. Despite everything that has happened, I can't leave her struggling to make ends meet on her own.

Glancing around the room, I take stock of everything I will have to move out. It's not a lot, but the emotional baggage I'm taking with me will make it seem that much harder. I still have her work schedule for the rest of the week, and I'm going to come back when I know she won't be here. Hopefully, my dad will be available to help me. Loathe as I am to move back into the apartment above the garage, it is probably what is best for now. At least, until I can get over Tiffany.

She didn't leave me a note, and though I want to let her know that I'll be okay, I don't leave her one either. She's made her decision. Allowing herself to have the freedom she thinks she needs. Instead, I walk out of the apartment and close the door quietly on this chapter of my life. Too bad this isn't like my favorite comic books, and I won't get the girl in the end.

TWENTY-FIVE

Tiffany

STELLA STANDS in front of me, finger pointing in my face as she goes on and on about all the ways I've royally fucked up. As if I didn't already know that. I regretted not saying anything the second he walked out the door.

"You're being a coward," she finishes her diatribe. That catches my attention.

"Excuse me?" I can't believe those words just came out of her mouth. "You ran over four hours away rather than talk to Johnny when you thought he had a thing for his ex."

"That's different," she scoffs and flips her hair over her shoulder. "I wasn't there permanently."

"No, Stella," I stand and she stumbles back. She should have known I wasn't going to sit there and let her call me a coward. "It's the same damn thing. The only difference is, I know I screwed up while you moped around on the sofa for a week."

"So you aren't here hiding out?"

She has me there, but that's not the full reason I'm here. "A tiny part is."

"And what is the other part?" Geez, I don't remember being this hard on her when she did the same thing.

"Regrouping," I nod, trying to convince myself as much as I am her. "I have to figure out what my next step needs to be."

"Does this mean you're going to fight for him?" Audrey finally joins the conversation. She's been sitting on the other end of the sofa letting Stella berate me. I wish I could say it wasn't normal, but it is. She doesn't do conflict and never has.

"Yes." And I'm going to. I don't have a choice. Spending my evenings with him rather than at a bar have been the highlights of my days. Being able to celebrate the little things and venting to him when I get home from work are what I look forward to most. Even his obsession with comics isn't enough to deter me from wanting him, no matter how hard I tried to fight it. All it did was make me like him more. Well, like may be an understatement. I fell for him. As much as my brain tried to fight it, my heart knew all along.

"That's it," Stella rolls her eyes. "The only answer you're going to give us is a *yes*. You don't have any plan?"

"Not yet," I reply. "But I'll figure something out." I have to, and it needs to be something big.

"ARE you sure this is a good idea right now?" Audrey asks when she notices the direction our Uber is heading. This plan calls for food and alcohol. Not a lot since that's why I'm in this mess. Well, that was the catalyst anyway.

"Yes," I answer, watching the buildings as we speed past them. "I'm sure."

"Shouldn't we be at home plotting your next move?" Stella pipes in, needing to add her two cents.

The driver stops in front of our favorite restaurant, and we all get out. The doors slamming closed one after the other. "That's what we're doing."

"That's funny because it looks like we're at our usual spot. Which is pointless." Audrey points to all the people standing outside, no doubt waiting for a table to open up. "There's no way we will get in there soon."

I laugh and reach for the handle on the door. "Don't worry. I've got that covered." The restaurant is packed and loud. Conversations blending together until I can't pick one out from the others. Leaving them behind, I walk to the hostess stand. "There should be a group of people waiting on me."

I'm happy to know that she doesn't have to ask my name despite me not coming in for a while. She glances around the dining area and nods her head. Pointing toward the back corner. "They are right back there. Let me grab you some menus and I'll lead you back."

I look over my shoulder to my cousins. They are patiently waiting by the door, but look at me like I'm wasting my time. The line behind me has doubled within the few moments I've been standing here. "Don't worry about that. I know my way through the place, and we can share menus with my friends. You look like you have your hands full."

She sighs in relief. "Thank you. Let me know if y'all need anything."

"Will do." I tap my hand on the stand twice before waving Audrey and Stella over.

When they are near me Stella whispers, "Is this some perk for being long-time customers?"

We weave between tables and people leaving until we come to a stop. "Nope," I beam, sweeping my hands in front of me at the table of new friends. "I've brought in reinforcements."

"Who are these people?" Audrey asks, her voice barely audible.

"Cosplayers, these are my cousins," I motion to my two best friends, and partners in crime. "Cousins, these are my friends from Comic-Con."

"When did you go to that?" Stella scrunches up her nose.

"Don't' worry about it. Right now… They are going to help me get my man back."

"ARE you sure this will fit me?" I stare at the latex costume doubting my entire plan. If I can't get that thing on, everything will fall apart. Audrey went by the apartment after we ate, and it didn't look like he'd even been there. I should have gone but I don't think I could have faced him on the off chance he was there.

"That girl, Rachel, said y'all were about the same size when I ran by her house to pick it up." Stella holds it up, inspecting the fabric. "It looks like an oversized condom to me."

"You are so ridiculous," I snatch it out of her hands. "It's not even see through."

"Maybe not, but it doesn't leave very much to the imagination." Audrey shakes her head. "Are you sure you want to leave the building in that?"

She has a point. I may not dress conservatively, but I've never worn something in public that could show off every single flaw that I have. Nerves over my plan take hold, and I sit down on the sofa. "I don't think I can do this."

"Oh no," Stella bends down in front of me. "You are not backing out. If you love him, and I'm pretty sure you do, you'll do whatever you need to get him back."

"I do lo—" the word gets caught in my throat. I've never uttered that word to anyone besides the people in my family. I take a deep breath then let it out. "I love him. He grounds me in a way that you two jerks never have."

"Hey," Stella yells. "We're the ones that usually bail your ass out of trouble."

She has a point. They've saved my ass more times than I can count. I'm just happy to have them by my side as I go to make a complete ass of myself. Hopefully Spencer will think it's endearing and take pity on me.

"Okay. Let's do this before I chicken out," my voice is confident, at least I hope it is. I look at the outfit dangling from Stella's hands and shake my head. I can't believe I'm going to do this. "Please tell me you have a robe for me to wear out of here."

TWENTY-SIX

Spencer

I PICK my phone up then set it back down. It's what I've been doing for the past twenty minutes. Totally normal, right? Maybe if I stare at the stupid thing long enough, it will ring or ding with a text message. *Something.* I half-hoped Tiffany would have called me by now. I could call her. Mom has told me more than once today to get over my pride and take the first step. I didn't do anything, though. Why is it my fault she can't accept my love?

No, my dumb ass would rather sit in a dark room and whine about her not freaking calling me. I should have left a note when I stopped by the apartment. She'd at least know I cared. I will need to text her eventually to let her know my part of the rent is taken care of until the lease is up. Even if it's not what I want.

"Honey," my mom comes into my room. "I love you, but can't you be gloomy in the garage apartment?"

Did I forget to mention that I'm in my childhood room? If that's not sad, I don't know what else is. I couldn't bring myself to stay in the space I lived in before Tiffany. That is where everything began between us. "Seriously? You're rejecting me now, too?"

"No, sweetheart," she sighs before turning on the light. "It's just that this isn't healthy. You obviously want to be with her."

"How do you know that?"

"You're sitting alone in the dark. In the room you grew up in." She pats my head like I'm a puppy that needs reassurance. "There's no better proof than that."

"What should I do?" I've always been able to think through problems logically and do what needed to be done. But I can't be logical when it comes to Tiffany.

"Well," Mom clears her throat. "If you love her, or want to make things work with her, then you need to go after her."

"What if she rejects me, again?" I'm not sure my heart can take it. Being with her has been like a game of tug of war. A constant push and pull but never knowing who will come out hurt. Not to mention I feel like a total loser coming to my mom for advice about my love life. How pathetic is it I don't have any close friends to talk about this shit with?

"It's something you'll have to accept. If you think she's worth fighting for, then go wait for her. She'll show up at your place, eventually."

I guess I need to go grab my bag. Tiffany is more than worth it, even if she drives me insane sometimes. "Thanks, Mom. That was what I needed to hear."

"Good luck," she calls to my retreating back.

I rush out of the house, flying right by Dad's confused stare. *Sorry, old man. I don't have time to stop and talk. I need to get my girl.* My feet pound up the stairs of the garage apartment, and I charge through the door. My bag is sitting on the sofa, still zipped closed. At least, I don't have to search for anything, except my keys. Where did I put those damn things?

I lift my laptop, shuffle around some papers, and then look around the room. They have to be here somewhere. No such luck. The sheets from the blow up mattress are thrown on the floor and the keys aren't on any of the flat surfaces. Oh well, looks like I will have to get an Uber to take me over there. In the main room, I lift my bag. Something shiny catches my eye, and my keys are right there. I guess I threw them down before I set the bag down when I came in. It doesn't surprise me. I was in a foul mood when I came in, and I didn't think I'd be able to get out of it. Thanks to my mom, I'm willing to put my heart on the line once again.

Grabbing the keys, I run out of the apartment and almost miss the second step on the stairs. Breaking my neck wouldn't help me convince Tiffany to stay with me. Though, it could help me in the sympathy department, but I don't want that to be the reason she sticks around.

With my keys in hand, I hit the fob to unlock the car doors, but headlights swing into the driveway. I lift my hands up to shield some of the brightness, trying to see who is walking toward me. "Spencer?" My heart lifts at the sound of her voice, and it takes everything in me not to rush to her and wrap her in my arms. She sought me out. This has to mean *something*.

"What are you doing here?" My words stop her in her tracks. I'm not sure if my tone was desperate or accusatory, but I want her to keep walking toward me. The car behind her turns the headlights off, but the orange parking lights are still glowing. Whoever brought her isn't leaving, and I have a sneaking suspicion it's one of her cousins.

"I, um," she pauses her words for a second and starts walking toward me again. A shadow coming into the light from the garage. "I wanted to talk to you."

Finally, I can see her. And holy shit. She's every nerd boy's wet dream. She's in a tight yellow and green suit. A black belt with an "X" in the middle wraps around her waist. She has a few strands of white hair clipped into her fiery mane. "You look…" I swallow hard. "Amazing. Is there a cosplay event happening somewhere I didn't know about?" Please don't say that you're coming here to break up with me then heading to an event I would love to go to.

"No," she smiles. That one gesture kills any doubt I have about her wanting to end things with me. There's no way she would smile if she was here to destroy my heart for a second time. "I asked Rachel if she had anything I could borrow that you would like. This is what she came up with. It's not complete since it was so last minute, but do you like it?"

"Like is an understatement." In reality, I want to haul ass up the steps to the apartment, and have my way with her on the blow up mattress.

"I just wanted to show you I lo—love you. I was a dumbass for pulling the shit I did. I was just scared."

"There are other ways to handle that fear. You know that, right?" She's still a couple of feet in front of me, and I need her to take those last few steps. To be within touching distance.

"Yes, I know that. But giving my heart to you had me questioning everything. I don't want to end up like Audrey. I love her to death, but she can be bitter when it comes to relationships. And well, if I give into you completely, I open myself up to that same hurt." She wraps her arms around herself. The one and only time I've ever seen her self-conscious of herself.

Rather than wait for her to come to me, I close the distance between us. Placing my hands on either side of her face and lifting her head until her eyes meet mine. "You don't have to be scared of that. I told you, I'm yours. I think I was yours that first night I met you at the concert. I'm not going anywhere. I just needed you to figure out what you wanted."

"I want you. Comics, cosplay and all. *You* make me happy. You make me feel more alive than bars or one-night stands ever could."

I laugh. I can't help it. "It's nice to know I rank above booze and sex." She's opening her mouth to argue her point but I crash mine down to hers. Not letting her say anything else. She had me when she said she loved me. Even more, when she said, I make her happy. Our tongues dance around each other, and this feels *right*. Like every-thing I've done my whole life has led me to this moment. To my happiness. "I'm here. For as long as you'll have me."

"What do you say we head home and *talk* more?" She winks at me and pulls me toward my car.

"That depends. How long do you get to keep the costume?"

Tiffany scrunches up her nose. "I have to get it back to Rachel, in perfect condition, tomorrow." She points at me and wags her finger, "So no funny business."

"I can't make any promises," a devilish grin sweeps across my face. I'm going to take full advantage of her dressed up as my favorite character. "But, yes, let's go home."

I walk around to the passenger side of the car and open

the door for her. She slides into the seat, trying her best to get comfortable in the skin-tight costume. I see my mom's shadow standing in the doorway and she waves. I wave back, grateful to know that she doesn't dislike my girl-friend. I throw my bag in the backseat and get in behind the wheel. "Are you sure about this?"

"There's nothing I've ever been more sure of." She grabs my hand on the gearshift, and squeezes it. That's all the confirmation I need. I'm ready to see where life takes me. Between the new design contract with Crooked Halo, and Tiffany back on my side, I feel like I've conquered the world.

Epilogue

THIS MAY BE the best concert I've ever been to in my life. I could kiss Spencer for getting tickets to ACL from his client. Let's be real, I probably will… repeatedly. For now, we'll sit at the back of the crowd and listen to the music roll over us. Normally I'd be in the thick of things at the front of the stage, but that's not where Spencer wants to be. This is better in every way possible. I may not be in the action, but I'm beside the one person who means the most to me.

Three months have passed since that night I showed up to his parent's house in costume, and I haven't looked back once. Am I still terrified of our future? You bet your ass, but I will not let my fear of getting hurt dictate my relationships anymore.

"I'm going to go get us some drinks," Spencer leans in to tell me. Even though we're nowhere near the stage, it's still loud as hell back here. "I don't want to miss them when they come on stage. Do you want anything?"

"Whatever you're having," I wink at him, remembering the night I met him. It feels like ages ago, now.

"Hurry back, though. You know how these people are when someone vacates a spot."

"I'll be right back." He gives me a loud, smacking kiss on the cheek and heads to the nearest beer stand.

I pull out my phone to see if I have any signal. Two little bars show on the strength and I sigh in relief.

Tiffany: Are you coming? We have a spot saved for you.

I've laid my backpack and blanket out on the ground just in case she shows up. The next band had an extra pass, and I knew I needed to drag her out of the house.

Audrey: Traffic is insane. I don't think I will be able to make it. Y'all have fun.
Tiffany: That's bullshit. You're in walking distance from us.
Audrey: I don't want to be the third wheel.
Tiffany: You won't be. You're my cousin!
Audrey: It's fine. I have some things I need to take care of, anyway.
Tiffany: Suit yourself. But don't say I didn't invite you to anything.
Audrey: Haha. Have fun and stay safe.
Tiffany: Will do.

I hate that she's holed herself away since Spencer and I have gotten more serious. It's like she's turned into me, except she's avoiding people in relationships entirely. It's not healthy. Oh, this is rich coming from me, the queen of one-night stands… Well, the former queen. I'm just happy to have found my person.

"Why are you frowning?" Spencer hands me a cup and sits down next to me. "That band wasn't so bad."

"Audrey."

"She's not coming, is she?" He scoots closer to me even though the fall air is still hot. "She'll get over whatever funk she's in."

"I know," I sigh. "I just wish she wouldn't keep blowing off plans when it's the both of us."

"You should go on more girl's nights with her. Just the two of you."

"I guess." The crowd ahead of us yells, and I know the big moment is finally upon us. I stand up with Spencer, trying to see over everyone's head. Geez, I hate being short. Finally, someone moves and I can see the logo Spencer created. He did an amazing job, and I can't wait to see the doors that open up to him now that he's designing for bands and companies.

Crooked Halo comes on stage and the crowd goes wild. Some of these people have never heard of them, but they've grown quite a following in the few months they've been performing. They got this gig because they are an up and coming local band. I'm just happy to know that I was one of their original fans.

The guitar and drums begin a rhythm and Dale is crooning about a guy and a girl who meet by chance. I like to think the song is about me and Spencer, but Dale will never confess it.

Chapter One: Audrey

I could be doing so many other things tonight. For instance, I could catch up on *Project Runway*. Or, I might even get caught up on my laundry. Hell, I could be washing my hair. But no. Instead, I'm sitting in a restaurant with these lovey-dovey couples planning Stella's wedding.

Don't get me wrong, I'm happy for my cousin. She finally let go of her weird obsession with work and started enjoying the little things in life. She's happier than she's ever been. I only wish it could have been us girls only.

Of course, wherever Tiffany goes, Spencer follows. That wild child found someone that keeps her leveled out. I never thought I'd see that day come. He's good for her, though.

While it fills me with joy to see my cousins so ridiculously in love, it makes me feel like the third wheel. I've been avoiding both of them for months. It's just hard seeing them glow because of their relationships when I can't seem to find anyone who completes me. Gah, could I sound any more like a sappy love movie? I haven't been truly happy since the day Justin dumped me our senior year of high school. I've gone on dates just to see if there is some sort of spark with anyone else, but they are all dull in comparison to him.

It's stupid to never move on, I know that. But I moved to this city in the hopes that maybe I'd run into him. Maybe with us being older and away from his dad, we could give things another go. My cousins thought it was because I wanted to be closer to them, and that's partly true. It's not the whole truth, though. I knew Justin was going to Hilltown University. I was supposed to go with him. We had our whole future planned out. It hurt too much then to go to the same college. I couldn't be in the same vicinity of the boy who destroyed my faith in relationships.

I hoped it would give me the space I needed to heal. To get over my high school sweetheart. It didn't. When Stella asked me if I wanted to be her roommate until we both got our feet beneath us, I jumped at the chance. I needed to get out of my town and all the memories I shared with Justin. The only way to do that was to start over completely.

Tiffany nudges me in the ribs with her elbow.

"What the hell is that for?" I whisper loud enough only for her to hear.

"Stella is talking about dresses. Get out of your head and pay attention."

Geez. When did she become so serious? I know this is important for both Johnny and Stella. I just don't understand why the planning has to be such a big production. Yes, it's important, but this could have been done at one of our apartments. Or, with just us girls. I'm really hoping there's more of that in the future. Not that I don't love Johnny and Spencer, but they are distracting from things that need to be done. And maybe I'm being a baby because I don't have anyone to cozy up to. This is all just too much.

It's a reminder of what could have been. What would have been if someone's parent wouldn't have gotten in the way. It pisses me off that his dad got married not long after Justin went off to college. He seemed lighter when I saw him around town. Where was all that understanding when his son was dating me? Why was I not good enough for his son to be with? Nope, my mind can't go there. Not tonight. I won't let.

"What do you think about burnt orange for your dresses?" Stella asks.

I haven't been listening, but that color definitely caught my attention. "Please don't make us be a college cliche," I whine. "If it's what you really want, I'll wear it, though." The color would look awful with Tiffany's hair. It makes sense that she would choose it since she wants a fall wedding. I hope she looks at other colors.

"I'll go ahead and mark it out. Y'all don't seem too excited about it," she sighs. "If you wouldn't have said anything, Tiff's face did."

The cousin in question bursts into laughter. "Who would have thought it'd be sweet Audrey that would object to that horrific color. She usually goes along with whatever." She's not wrong. I'm very go with the flow…to an extent. I don't like surprises, and tend to stick to myself. Okay so I'm nothing like Tiffany. Maybe that's what's wrong with me.

Nope. Not going down that road again. It's not a good headspace to be in. Why the hell does Justin keep popping into my thoughts? Is it because Stella is getting what I should have already had? My fairytale, happily ever after.

I need to get out of this mood. If I don't, I won't be any help to her or anyone else.

Even though I'm alone and not completely happy, I can't help but feel excited for Stella. This is something I never thought I'd see with her. At least, not for a very long time. Men weren't even on her radar until she met Johnny. But I need a break from the stolen kisses and planning. "I'll be right back."

I walk toward the back of the restaurant so they know I'm not leaving. The restroom is the closest escape I can think of. The chatter from the patrons is barely audible as I close the restroom door. Finally, peace and quiet. I know Tiffany means well, but she didn't have to call me out like that in front of Stella. I refuse to be the third wheel. The realization that most people take dates to weddings finally dawns on me. Crap, I'm going to have to find a date. Maybe I can ask someone in accounting to come as my plus one. It's not ideal but I don't see myself finding my soulmate between now and Stella's wedding.

My reflection in the mirror is pale, and I look exhausted. I've basically turned into Stella. Well, the Stella that existed before she went to Asheville. I've thrown myself into work and doing things around my apartment. Anything to keep me occupied and not have to go out with Tiffany and Spencer.

Minutes pass by and I'm still not ready to go back out there. If I don't, someone will come barging in looking for me. Tiffany and Stella have zero patience, especially if they think I'm acting weird. I step back through the door. My gaze on my feet as I walk through the restaurant to the table.

Someone blocks my path and I slam into them. Liquid splashes all over me, the person, and the floor. Shit, and now I've knocked someone's drink out of their hand. "I'm so sorry," I say before I look up. My eyes meet warm brown eyes I could never forget, and I gasp. No way. There's no way in hell I would run into him...here. But here he is. The guy who broke my heart all those years ago and who I still see in my dreams to this day. It's as if my thoughts conjured him.

"Audrey?" My name spills from his lips and all I can think about is the way we used to lie on the hood of his car and stare at the stars. Talking about our futures.

I can't do this. Not tonight. Not ever. I thought he moved to Dallas for fuck's sake. He's not supposed to be here anymore. I don't bother going back to the table. I'm running through the restaurant and out the front door. Stella and Tiffany calling my name before the door cuts off their voices.

Acknowledgments

I had so much fun writing Gone Nerdy. And it wouldn't have been possible without the support of those around me. Tasha & Kelsie, you two have heard me bitch and moan when I felt like giving up. Y'all are the real MVPs. Thank you for letting me figure crap out with y'all. Nessa, I love you and can't imagine a world without you as my best friend. Aurora, thank you for keeping me on track and making sure I get my stuff done.

My Alphas… you ladies rock. You have no idea how much your help means to me. Seriously, y'all read it when it's ugly and encourage me to keep going with your messages.

Victoria, thank you for polishing this beauty up. Your insight means so much to me. Sly Fox Cover Designs, thank you for having the perfect cover for my spunky red-head.

Mom and Dad, just thank you for everything.

Hubs, Boy Child & Wee One, I love y'all to the moon and back. Y'all sacrifice more than anyone when I'm on deadline.

Dreamers, thank you for sticking with me each book and answering my crazy questions every day. I love our little group, and y'all make my days brighter.

Readers, thank you for reading this. You're the reason I do what I do.

About the Author

Katrina Marie lives in the Dallas area with her husband, two children, and fur baby. She is a lover of all things geeky. When she's not writing you can find her at her children's sporting events, or curled up reading a book.
Visit her online: katrinamarieauthor.com
Sign up for her newsletter http://bit.ly/KatrinaMarieNewsletter

facebook.com/KatrinaMarieAuthor
twitter.com/katrmarieauthor
instagram.com/katrinamarieauthor
bookbub.com/profile/katrina-marie